Fire at Sea

The Mysterious Tragedy of the *Morro Castle*

*Also by Thomas Gallagher
and published by The Lyons Press:*

ASSAULT IN NORWAY

Fire at Sea

The Mysterious Tragedy of the *Morro Castle*

by Thomas Gallagher

THE LYONS PRESS
Guilford, Connecticut
An imprint of The Globe Pequot Press

The Lyons Press is an imprint of The Globe Pequot
Press

10 9 8 7 6 5 4 3 2 1

Printed in the United States of America

ISBN 1-58574-624-X

Library of Congress Cataloging-in-Publication Data is
available on file.

To my friend Ray Robinson

AUTHOR'S NOTE

The material for this book was compiled from documents in the National Archives in Washington, D.C.; from prison files and police- and fire-department records; from the personal accounts of passengers and crew given under oath during the Steamboat Inspectors' Investigation in the Custom House in New York in September, 1934; and from the Dickerson Hoover Report, based on the Custom House testimony and prepared for the United States Department of Commerce in October, 1934.

The twelve volumes of testimony taken during the

trial, in 1935-36, of the ship's officers, were made available from a private source and proved to be of invaluable help. Last and most important of all were the letters from survivors and the direct interviews with them in cities ranging from Los Angeles, California, to Trenton, New Jersey, where, in 1956, Chief Radio Operator George W. Rogers was met face to face and questioned in the New Jersey State Penitentiary.

All direct quotes and the material in parentheses appearing in the book derive from these sources.

Fire at Sea
The Story of the *Morro Castle*

Fire at Sea

1

On Wednesday afternoon, September 5, 1934, the *Morro Castle,* a twin-screw turbo-electric liner regarded as the last word in marine construction, one of the safest and most modern vessels afloat, steamed out of Havana harbor and put to sea. She had left New York September first on a Labor Day cruise to Cuba and this was her return voyage. Aboard were over 200 officers and crew and more than 300 passengers, and of the latter many waved as the ship passed its namesake, historic Morro Castle, gray and alone in the sun's downpour above Havana's waters.

Passengers always thrill to the sea closing around them. The gliding away of land, the growing instability of the elements, the falling away of gulls and the tensioning of masts and lanyard lines add zest to the incongruity of their having the land still with them. Within the hull-bound community are luxury staterooms, bars, sumptuous dining rooms, lounges, ballrooms and orchestras, the best of food, the most obsequious service. Men in pongee and women in linen, college boys and pig-tailed little girls—all respond to a sense of achievement and danger. They are conquerors fresh out of a travel bureau, Vikings with glass between them and the salt spray.

Here and there, they see seamen coiling rope, scrubbing, polishing; a solitary figure at the bow, painting numbers and diagrams on deck for shuffleboard. But men who live on ships look different, their language is different, their faded denims and dry, cauterized faces tend to make them invisible except to one another. They are outsiders in the city that they keep moving through the water, withdrawn from observation by the nature of their function.

The seamen live forward, in the fo'c'sle, through which runs a maze of rivets, steampipes and nationalities, and where weeks of close living, the smells of grease, sweat, stale cigarettes and a stench from old shoes web the air and make it hard to breathe; where work clothes, draped over the iron piping of the bunks, over the doors of lockers, over anything that can be used as a support, make of the already cramped space a kind of hacked-out jungle clearing. It is only a matter of time before the jungle grows back, to be hacked away again; and before the consumption of liquor, card-playing and petty thefts flare into fist fights and knifings.

The stewards, musicians, porters, waiters, bartenders and messboys, however, deal directly with the customer, play requested medleys during dances, see the deb before she puts on her make-up, help the intoxicated poltroon to bed at night, concoct seasick remedies for dowagers, and deliver sandwiches and coffee to devotees of bridge and poker. They know the passengers and the passengers know them.

Captain Robert Wilmott, master of the *Morro Castle,* had been with the Ward Line for thirty-one years. He was a large rotund man, almost cherubic in roundness and skin coloring; but on this trip his face had taken on a scowling vigilance behind which could be seen fear and an inner scrambling to pin down that fear. They were only two hours out of Havana when he called Chief Radio Operator Rogers into his cabin.

"Now, Mr. Rogers, you are my chief operator and I

can talk to you, man to man. You appear to be an intelligent person. What is the matter with your second radio officer, Alagna? I think the man is crazy."

"Why, sir?"

"We've always had trouble with this man, but now this has happened: Second Officer Freeman was on watch and rang for the radio compass, in accordance with my orders.

"Alagna rang the bridge with two bells (ordinarily my signal) and sent a message to Freeman, who was then running the ship, telling him not to use the radio compass so damn much and stop tuning in music on it.

"I want that man removed in New York. . . . He is a detriment to the service and I'm going to see to it that the Radiomarine Corporation of America gives him no more posts in the American Merchant Marine."

Two months before, Alagna ("I was just out of college and the food revolted me," he says today) had tried to get the other officers on the *Morro Castle* to sign a petition for better food and better working conditions. After being refused by the officers (Freeman among them), Alagna had gone on strike just as the ship, filled with passengers and cargo, was preparing to leave New York. He and the other junior operator held the ship up for two hours until a special agreement—more money and better working conditions—was signed by the company. The men returned to work and the ship sailed; the company never lived up to the agreement and never intended to.

"Another thing," Captain Wilmott went on, "I want you to take the key to that emergency room and keep it in your pocket. Don't leave it where Alagna can get at it. I don't trust him. He is vengeful. Before we left Havana he said there were ways of getting even with the ship."

The foregoing conversation is based only on Rogers's version of it and there is reason to believe that if Wilmott used words to this effect in Rogers's presence, he used them not against Alagna but against Rogers himself. On September fifth, when the conversation took place, Rogers had been Chief Radio Operator of the *Morro Castle* for less than a month. He had previously been a junior operator on the ship, and the circumstances leading to his promotion, on August eleventh, would have made it necessary for him to reproduce the above conversation as he did.

Rogers lived in Bayonne, New Jersey, where a friend of his, Preston Dillenbeck, was studying to become a maritime radio operator. Rogers told Dillenbeck in July, a month before the August promotion, that he was Chief Radio Operator of the *Morro Castle* and might be able to get Dillenbeck a post on the ship as one of his junior operators. At that time Rogers was a junior operator under Chief Radio Operator Stanley Ferson, and the reason for the falsehood becomes clear from the following letter sent by Rogers to Dillenbeck on July 24, 1934, from Havana, Cuba, while Rogers was aboard the ship as a junior operator.

Dear Pres:

Was in New York last Saturday but didn't get a chance to see you. Well OM how goes everything in Bayonne? This is my second trip and everything's going along very nicely. How is the code practice getting along? Suppose that service work is keeping you very busy these days. Well, don't forget the fact that you need that 2nd class license.

One of our juniors is in a jam with the Federal Radio Commission and I hate to see the fellow get in a lot of trouble. It has to do with the sending of a CQ message for the Radio Telegraphists' Union without authority and this, of course, comes under the heading of false and fraudulent signals. There is a way that I can help him and at the same time pave the way for you so I want you to do the following.

I am enclosing a letter that I have written and I want you to rewrite this letter on your typewriter and address it in a plain envelope to the address that I will give you. Then take the letter to New York and mail it from there. This is very important. Rewrite the letter on your typewriter, address it in a plain envelope and mail it in New York. This will tip him off as to what to expect and at the same time, having been mailed in New York when I am in Cuba, it will not involve me.

When I get to New York I will get another junior who will be assigned to the ship temporarliy so that when you get your ticket there will be no trouble getting you assigned here with me. This must be done as soon as you receive this letter so that he will get the letter in New York when we arrive there. Don't fail me, please. Will try to see you this trip.

George

The letter that Dillenbeck copied and unwittingly sent was not to one of the junior operators but to the Chief Radio Operator. It follows in full:

Mr. Stanley Ferson
Radio Operator SS Morro Castle
c/o Ward Line SS Company
Foot of Wall Street
New York, N. Y.
Dear Sir:
  During the past several weeks the writer of this letter has handled communications from various parties that lead him, in the spirit of fairness, to advise you of the following:
  As you probably know, there is an action being taken against you by the Ward Line with the Federal Radio Commission. This action is, primarily, to discipline you for your action in the recent Morro Castle disturbance. Reports are received from the Morro Castle every voyage regarding your attitude toward the company and these reports are being compiled in the final summation of your case.

The writer has known you for the complete time that you have been on the Morro Castle and, in order to avoid the approaching unpleasantness, I would advise you that you do the following:

Send in your resignation as operator on the Morro Castle and apply to the Radio Corporation of America for an indefinite leave of absence. This will remove you from the jurisdiction of the Ward Line, who then, from what I have learned, will, necessarily drop their action against you.

As long as you stay clear of the Ward Line vessels you will be all right.

Personally, I have watched your struggle with the causes of your disagreement with the Ward Line and I think that they have complaints that have been just.

For obvious reasons the writer must remain unknown to you although you know him very well.

I don't like to see anyone framed as they are evidently doing to you.

I am sure the above course of action is best for all and will, undoubtedly, result in all action against you being dropped.

Trusting that the above will be received in the same spirit that it was written the writer remains,

A Friend

Pres—Send this letter to the address at the head of the letter. Write it on a plain piece of typewriter paper and use a plain envelope and mail it in New York.

George

On July thirty-first, Rogers sent another, stronger and more urgent letter from Cuba for Dillenbeck to copy and send to Stanley Ferson, and on August 11, 1934, Ferson resigned as Chief Radio Operator of the *Morro Castle*. Rogers, who was next in line, thereupon became chief radio operator and George Alagna became second.

Now in July, when Rogers had first boarded the *Morro Castle* as a junior operator, he had told Alagna that he'd been assigned to the ship to act as a stool pigeon for the Radiomarine Corporation of America. "I'm supposed to obtain information which will lead to Ferson's dismissal. And yours, too."

The two anonymous letters strengthened this fabrication because when Ferson discussed them with Alagna before resigning, Rogers told Alagna that they had been sent to Ferson by J. B. Duffy, Superintendent of the Radiomarine Corporation of America. "I've obtained no information on you, though," Rogers added. "Nothing that will affect you in any way."

On September fifth, therefore, when Captain Wilmott called Rogers into his office, the latter had already reached the point where continued success meant more of the same duplicity. It was true that Stanley Ferson had had some difficulty with the Ward Line, and Rogers used this truth to give credence to his two anonymous letters, urging Ferson to resign. It was also true that

Alagna had both gone on strike and argued with Ivan Freeman about the radio compass, and Rogers used these two truths to make Alagna the object of Captain Wilmott's growing fears and suspicions.

Captain Wilmott was a company man, as all sea captains should be, and conducted his affairs both in port and aboard ship to the best advantage of the owners. His job was to bring the *Morro Castle,* with its machinery, cargo, passengers, equipment and crew, safely and expeditiously to port, so that the voyage would be as profitable as possible for the owners. Such a captain must understand stowage, how to separate cargo so that combustibles can be easily jettisoned in the event of fire. He must be a businessman and something of a lawyer; must understand marine insurance and know how to salvage a vessel. In addition, he must be an expert navigator equal to any emergency, a disciplinarian and something of a hypocrite—possessor of split-level graces that will attract both the old and the new rich as passengers.

It is no wonder, then, that systematized worry is one of the occupational hazards among captains of large vessels. Their greatest satisfaction comes not from the money they make, which falls far short of being commensurate with the responsibilities, but from their position of absolute command which, in turn, adds to their worry. The seamen under command have no real loyalty to the captain and he knows it; they have no loyalty to the ship or to the shipping company.

To make matters worse, the *Morro Castle*'s sailing schedule was such that for over two hundred members of the crew the ship was virtually a prison. She would arrive every Saturday morning, discharge passengers and cargo, take on supplies and fuel, load more passengers and cargo, and be steaming toward Havana again that same evening. As a result, only Captain Wilmott and a few of the major officers were ever given vacations. The minor officers and crew had to sign off the ship—quit their jobs—if they wanted time off.

"They never dun nothin' for me," is a refrain that runs as endlessly through the fo'c'sle as the hiss of steam and the clatter of the agate plates from which the men eat. It is an occupation that breeds insecurity, anger and resentment, and yet, ironically, an occupation during the working hours of which a carefully planned "accident" can wipe out the profits of several voyages.

2

As the ship sailed on, Captain Wilmott's fears grew to a point where even the passengers began to take notice. He was "persistently absent from all meals, so that at the captain's table there sat only emptiness and silence throughout the voyage," Rosario Comacho, a passenger from Cuba, said. "As rumor had it through the entire voyage, this was because of serious trouble of some kind in relation to the crew."

On Thursday evening, September sixth, Captain Wilmott told a passenger with whom he'd become friendly that "his first act on reaching New York would be to fire Chief Radio Operator Rogers, that Rogers was capable of acts which might endanger both the passengers and the ship." He had to be gotten rid of immediately, Wilmott said, before the ship made another run.

Information had reached the captain that two bottles, one of sulphuric acid and one of a foul-smelling liquid, had been brought aboard in Havana. Whether this information was the basis for Wilmott's remarks to his passenger friend is not known, but the next morning, on Friday, September seventh, Wilmott called Rogers into his quarters and asked him about the two bottles. Rogers admitted having this conversation with the captain ("Wilmott called me into his office the first thing Friday morning, before I went on watch.") but was vague as to what had transpired.

"There was a lot of talk in Havana that if things didn't pan out there were ways of getting even," he said. "I repeated these things to the captain and told him that I'd thrown it [*a* bottle] overboard. I merely reported to him that I'd disposed of it." (George Rogers used the singular in referring to what he'd thrown overboard. According to him, there was one bottle, not two.)

Shortly after this conversation between Wilmott and Rogers, Wilmott called Chief Officer William F. Warms into his office and completely reversed his suspicions of the night before.

"Wilmott called me into his quarters on Friday

morning," Chief Officer Warms said. "He told me he was very worried that something would happen. He said he could feel it; that he had definite information that Alagna had two bottles and that Rogers had taken them away from him. The captain said he was afraid Alagna would harm him and he kept his door locked."

In reply to the suggestion that they "put Alagna in irons," Warms quoted Wilmott as saying, "No, we'll get rid of him in New York. I don't want any trouble with him. He held the ship up once, an hour and forty-five minutes."

"Let me search his quarters, then," Warms said.

"No, he's too damn smart to keep anything there. Just keep an eye on him today and tonight."

This conversation definitely took place after Wilmott's conversation with Rogers, because Chief Officer Warms, who had the four-to-eight watch on the bridge, would not have been called into the captain's quarters until after he had come off watch, or until after Wilmott's conversation with Rogers, whose watch in the radio room started at eight (eight to twelve). Wilmott must therefore have obtained his added information from Rogers and, moreover, been convinced that Rogers was telling the truth.

Later the same day, Wilmott had the following conversation with Fourth Officer Howard Hansen.

"I've been told that Rogers found two bottles, one of

acid and one of a bad-smelling fluid," Wilmott said. "And I've heard that Alagna threatened to throw the fluid in the lounge on the last night out so passengers could not board the ship for the next voyage."

In Havana, before the ship's departure, a drunken sailor from the steamship *President Wilson* had said something about how to "get even" with a ship. Several members of the *Morro Castle* crew remembered this man explaining how a certain kind of stench bomb, thrown in the public rooms of a ship as she neared her home port, would cause the loss of thousands of dollars to the company because of delayed sailing dates, as well as a less calculable loss of reputation.

"Captain," Hansen said, "if you're afraid of Alagna, why not lock him up?"

"No, that's not necessary. The bottles have been thrown overboard."

No one saw Rogers find the bottles or throw them overboard, however, and if Captain Wilmott had proof that one of them contained sulphuric acid, Rogers would have said precisely what he did say. He would again have taken a verifiable truth—the drunken sailor from the SS *President Wilson* talking about how to get even —and used it to throw suspicion on Alagna, to eradicate the word "acid," and, most importantly, to reduce "two" bottles to "one."

"There was no acid," he said. "There was a bottle of

stink-ball fluid. It smelled, so I threw it overboard."

No one on the ship and no Ward Line official knew it at the time, but George W. Rogers was a psychopath with a criminal record dating back twenty years. According to one of several subsequent psychiatric reports, all of which agreed diagnostically, he was a "sociopathic personality; a shrewd individual who attempts to manipulate his environment."

Highly intelligent but lacking even a child's judgment, an expert dissembler of facts, motives and intentions, he had always, despite his record, managed to ingratiate himself anew. The very man he had defrauded of a job, former Chief Radio Operator Stanley Ferson, had shaken his hand before leaving the ship. George Alagna found him glib and convivial; J. B. Duffy of the Radiomarine Corporation of America thought very highly of him.

Now Rogers was aware that the friction between the radio room and bridge, well known among the ship's officers, dated back to before his *Morro Castle* assignment by the Radiomarine Corporation of America. The bringing aboard of sulphuric acid in Havana could therefore be imputed to his assistant, George Alagna, the young collegiate hothead who had openly expressed his belief in unionism and already gotten himself in trouble because of that belief.

In 1934 the Communist movement was feasting on

both the depression and the retrenchments of big business. Any attempt like Alagna's to get other officers to sign a petition for better food and working conditions would naturally be looked upon with great suspicion. Rogers knew that the step from "strike organizer" to "saboteur" would be taken without any added help from him.

On the afternoon before the *Morro Castle* was to dock in New York, Captain Wilmott had as his guests four passengers from cabins just below the bridge on A deck: Dr. Charles Cochrane, Chief of the Urological Staff of Kings County Hospital in Brooklyn, the doctor's sister, Catherine Cochrane, and Dr. Theodore Vosseler and his wife. Wilmott had more than acid to worry him as he led his guests into his quarters, for he knew that a hurricane was moving up from the Caribbean, that he would in any case have to be on the bridge long before dawn to bring the ship into New York, and that twelve hours later he would be outward bound.

And yet the hurricane must have given him a desperately needed object for his fears, for throughout the visit he kept telling his guests of the experience he had had the year before, when he'd piloted the ship ("lost" to the company for two days because the radio apparatus had broken down) through a hurricane off Hatteras with no more damage than a few wet blankets.

"The bridge is sixty-five feet above water level, and there were times when I couldn't see over the tops of the waves towering over and inundating the bow."

He showed them the watch the passengers had given him at a dinner in his honor afterwards. It bore the inscription: "In recognition of superb seamanship through a most perilous hurricane—Sept. 13-18, '33."

That evening, Captain Wilmott did not attend the traditional farewell dinner. "We were confident of his presence," Rosario Comacho said, "inasmuch as word had gone round that he'd promised a close friend among the passengers that he would be with us this one evening for the traditional Captain's Dinner. And there we were, waiting dinner. People were becoming outspoken and disgruntled, when an announcement informed us that Captain Wilmott would not dine with us due to unforeseen circumstances."

Captain Wilmott had again decided to dine alone in his cabin. He had ordered a tray of food brought up from the galley by the same waiter who always served him and, after the waiter had left, was eating a tropical melon, crates of which had been taken on at Cuba, when he buckled over and seized his stomach.

Whether the food or coffee had been tampered with in the galley, or in the elevator on the way up from the galley, is not known. The ice water in the captain's thermos, already in the cabin when the waiter arrived, might have been adulterated earlier that afternoon. A poisonous pill or capsule might have been substituted for one that the captain, who suffered from indigestion, was in the habit of taking.

A few minutes later, First Officer Warms was entering his cabin to get his pipe when Dr. De Witt Van Zile, the ship's chief surgeon, told him the captain was sick. Warms, who knew of the captain's high blood pressure, considered him a "very nervous man" and often talked to him in an effort to "calm him down," stepped into the captain's cabin and said, "What is it, Bob?"

"Something I've eaten. I don't know. I'll take an enema and be all right." He made a motion with his hand for Warms to get back to the bridge, "Go on. I'll be fine in a minute."

About an hour later, Fourth Officer Howard Hansen found Captain Wilmott in his bathtub. "He was partly undressed and there was no water in the tub. I called for help, meanwhile working his arms back and forth."

Quartermaster Samuel Hoffman heard Hansen's call, hurried to the captain's quarters and helped carry the rotund mariner to his bed. While they were working over him, Robert Tolman, the purser, came in ("Captain Wilmott was quite blue") and was followed by Dr. Van Zile, who immediately put a stethoscope to the captain's chest and prepared a hypodermic needle. The Chief Steward, Henry Speierman, then came in, and after him Chief Engineer Eban S. Abbott, First Engineer Anthony Bujia, Second Steward James Pond and Watchman Joseph O'Connor.

They stayed outside in the captain's office until the doctor came out and said, "The captain is dead. He's been dead for some time."

Chief Officer Warms was still on duty on the bridge, and in his absence a conversation took place during which the remark was made, "We have one four-striper left." Chief Engineer Abbott was the four-striper referred to (Chief Officer Warms had three stripes) and in view of subsequent events this conversation is very interesting. For though it is true that only a deck officer can take over command of a ship when a captain dies, the remark, if it expressed anything, expressed a doubt as to Chief Officer Warms's ability to take over.

"No one had much confidence in Warms," Fourth Officer Howard Hansen said, "and I wondered at the time if we would make it [to New York]. However, all of us officers on the bridge held a Master's License and any one of us could have brought the ship home."

Assistant Steward James Pond thought otherwise. "Warms was a real sailor. There was something rough about him but that goes with a real seadog type. I was prepared to go anywhere under his command. I had confidence in him. I'm talking about his ability as a sailor, not his social status on the ship."

Chief Officer Warms did not hear the remark about four- and three-stripers, not firsthand, that is, but when the Purser, Robert Tolman, went to Warms on the bridge and said, "I've prepared papers, placing you as master and Ivan Freeman Chief Officer," Warms told him, "Go below and tell everyone you see that I'm the master and to obey my orders."

Robert Tolman then wrote two radiograms for Warms. The first was to Thomas S. Torresson, the Ward Line's Marine Superintendent, and the second to Victor M. Seckendorf, the company's Traffic Passenger Manager. Tolman would have informed Henry E. Cabaud, the Ward Line's vice president, but the latter's address happened to be in Wilmott's safe and Tolman didn't remember it.

The first radiogram read:

WILMOTT DECEASED 7:45 P.M. ACKNOWLEDGE
WARMS

Some time later, the following radiogram, addressed to Robert Tolman, was received by the *Morro Castle:*

PLEASE CONFIRM QUICKLY MESSAGE SENT BY WARMS TO SECKENDORF REGARDING WILMOTT GIVING DETAILS
WARDLINE
10:28 P

Tolman was being asked, in short, to confirm and elucidate an unnecessarily cryptic message, and asked by Seckendorf himself, who was no doubt cursing Warms for being so damned mysterious. The remark about four- and three-stripers immediately after Wilmott's death, followed by Warms's order to Tolman, "Go below and tell everyone you see that I'm master and to obey my orders," apparently did not so much cause dissension as bring it to the surface.

Mrs. Wilmott said later that Captain Wilmott had told her, "Warms is too erratic. I don't want him on the ship. He doesn't know what he's doing from one moment to the next."

And now here was Seckendorf, a businessman, going over the head of the man in command of the ship to ask another businessman, the purser, to explain things to him.

This time Tolman sent the message that should have been sent in the first place, and this time he signed his own name to it.

Confirming message from Warms Stop Wilmott deceased acute indigestion and heart attack seven forty-five this evening Stop All papers for entry in order.

Tolman Purser

The death of a captain at sea is not unlike the death of a President during a war. In the dining room, the buzzers and bells that always accompany the final celebration died down and the colored streamers flying from table to table drifted to the floor. Passengers spoke in lower tones or left the dining room altogether as the loudspeaker announced that the ball that was to have rounded out the cruise would be canceled.

A Cuban group among the passengers, however, had already gathered on the game deck aft for the Captain's Ball. Rafael Mestre, a young student from Santiago, had fetched some rhumba records and maracas from Rosario Comacho's stateroom and was playing them on the recording machine in anticipation of the orchestra's arrival. Suddenly the music stopped and an officer, appearing on the bandstand with upraised hands, told his startled listeners that the captain had passed away and that there would be no music in the public rooms of the ship for the remainder of the voyage.

Decks and public rooms were soon deserted as passengers, upset by the news, besieged by rumors and giving way to irrational fears, concentrated on packing for a quick departure in the morning. Others, only momentarily bereaved by the death of a man they had never seen, pooled their Cuban rum and made an Irish wake of it in stateroom after stateroom. It was as if the ship, her wind-swept decks deserted except for drunken stragglers here and there, were sliding aimlessly through the sea.

Meanwhile, in the captain's cabin, Warms, Dr. Van Zile and Chief Engineer Eban S. Abbott were tense and silent as the captain was dressed and laid out. Assistant Steward James Pond, who had had experience with shipboard deaths, had offered his mortuary services because "someone had to do it and it didn't bother me."

Chief Engineer Abbott especially, an old friend of Wilmott's, who had heard the sulphuric-acid story and knew that the captain had been locking himself in his cabin at night, was visibly nervous and moved. The ship had carried guns and ammunition (listed in the manifest as "sporting goods") to one of the factions in the Cuban revolution, and Havana this trip had been a little unnerving because of it. Just the previous year the ship had been caught in crossfire between a Cuban gunboat and a fort overlooking the harbor, and Abbott vividly remembered the sounds of those bullets ricocheting off the decks and superstructure.

Now his best friend on the ship was dead, from acute indigestion, heart attack, or poison. To this day the cause is conjecture, for the tray of food was never examined, and neither was the drinking water or any medicine or box of pills in the medicine chest. Except for the tray of food, which was eventually removed and brought back down to the galley, the captain's cabin and outer office was left untouched. The ship was approaching New York where a thorough examination of the captain's body would be made and the cause of death definitely determined.

That examination was never to take place, though according to Dr. Van Zile, whose examination was admittedly superficial and who also failed to reach New York alive, the death "was probably due to cardiac insufficiency."

"Captain Wilmott did not have any marks of violence or foul play," Fourth Officer Howard Hansen said. "His face was black or discolored. He suffered from a heart ailment and could have died from that, but I have reason to think that he was given a Micky Finn which could have brought on a heart attack."

3

Warms returned to the bridge after Wilmott's body had
been laid out and the radiograms sent. Being Chief
Mate, he had immediately informed the other officers
and assumed command of the ship. The ship's second
officer, Ivan Freeman, was promoted to first officer;
Third Officer Clarence Hackney became second; and
Fourth Officer Howard Hansen became third. All four
of these men held licenses as masters of vessels of unlimited tonnage. Indeed, because of the depression and
the scarcity of jobs, several members of the crew from

the bo'sun down held mate's tickets, and one merchant-marine officer, Arthur J. Pender, was working on the ship as a night watchman.

The air was very busy thereafter, as is usually the case with a shipboard death, and at midnight Chief Radio Operator Rogers was relieved by Third Operator Charles Maki.

At 2:30 A.M., seven hours after Wilmott's death, Acting Captain Warms was still on duty on the bridge. At once exhausted and unable to relax, he felt a throbbing chronic potential in the ship beneath him. Her spine, sliding straight beneath the sea, was his to straddle; he had the feel of her and he knew he was the master. This was his life, the sea; he had shipped out thirty-seven years before as a cabin boy, had later joined the navy and advanced to bo'sun second class before his discharge. He had received his master's license in 1918, after which time he'd commanded several freighters for the Ward Line, owners of this ship he was taking into quarantine. Though he had never mastered a passenger liner with a vast superstructure such as the *Morro Castle's*, his present master's license was for unlimited tonnage upon the waters of any ocean, and he was a licensed pilot for New York Bay and Harbor. The idea of more responsibility added to his belief in himself; he looked over his shoulder at the shimmering phosphorescent streak following the ship and felt a new pleasurable direction to his life.

Only two things marred the feeling: his fatigue (he had not slept for thirty hours) and the dirty weather ahead. He glanced round at the smoke running hard off the stack to port quarter. Then he squinted into the wind, as if in appraisal of its obscure source, its scope, its hidden strength, and prepared himself, in the manner of sea captains everywhere, to resent it. It was a "north-easter," the bane of vacationers along these Jersey beaches—wet, lashing and seemingly endless.

They were only thirty miles south of Scotland Light; they would soon be turning into Ambrose Channel and the safety of New York Harbor. Quarantine in a matter of hours.

Two decks below the bridge, Daniel Campbell, assistant steward, was cleaning up in the smoking room. There was a party of four there drinking highballs: Una Cullen and her escort, Mae Maloney and a second gentleman, who kept alternating his attention between this party and another in the lounge. The dance that was to have rounded out the cruise had been canceled after Wilmott's death, but several couples had already dressed by then, and these two were among them. Misses Cullen and Maloney were wearing long trailing evening gowns; the men, their white starched fronts like breastplates against the depression in America, double-breasted tuxedos with the jackets unbuttoned and played out over the arms of their chairs.

"Quarter to three," one of the men said, looking at the clock.

Steward Daniel Campbell overheard him and said, "But it's really a quarter to four, shore time."

"No, no," the man, who had been drinking rather heavily, said, "it is only a quarter to three."

"But at quarantine tomorrow the clocks are going ahead," Campbell insisted. "The time is really a quarter to four."

The men had brought their own liquor to the smoking room (rum costing only four dollars a gallon in Havana) and Campbell had been serving them setups. Tips were poor on the northbound trip for this reason, and Campbell wanted to get rid of them. Besides, he had work to do; the whole place had to be gone over with the electric buffing machine for the new group of passengers tomorrow.

("The passengers go ashore in Havana," Campbell explained later. "They get this rum there very cheap, and those who have been moderate become hard drinkers. They get into a room with a gallon on the table and call for White Rock.")

"If you're planning to get some sleep before we dock," he said, "you'd better get to bed."

"I'm not going to bother going to bed," Una Cullen said, and the others agreed.

Then, at exactly 2:50 ship's time, Paul Arneth, a butcher from Brooklyn, came in and, with his back to the laughing and drinking foursome, asked Campbell in a whisper if there was a fire on board.

"I smell smoke," he said.

Campbell placed his tray on the table and hurried toward the lounge. There had been rumors among the late drinkers of "wastebasket" fires; and about an hour earlier Arthur Bagley and Jerry Dunn, both seamen, had seen a number of drunken passengers in the writing room tossing lighted cigarettes into a wastebasket. The seamen urged them to stop, but the passengers, in the time-honored manner of drunks, had expressed complete command of the situation.

This story was corroborated by passenger James A. Flynn, who claimed that he discovered a fire in the writing room at 2:10 exactly. He had been sitting with Miss Ann Conroy of Philadelphia on B deck when a smell of smoke attracted his attention. He got up, discovered a small fire in the writing room (the cigarette tossers had vanished) and reported it to a steward. He did not report it to Campbell but to some other steward, probably

Sydney Ryan, who was also on duty. At that time the fire was so small that he then returned to his deck chair next to Miss Conroy to take up where he'd left off.

When Campbell reached the lounge at 2:50, he found a party drinking brandy but causing no disturbance. He then started toward the writing room, which was just forward of the lounge on the same promenade deck.

Back on the bridge, Night Watchman Foersch was making the report to Acting Captain Warms: "Captain, I smell and see smoke."

"Where?" Warms said. It was raining and he and Second Officer Hackney had been looking for Sea Girt Light.

"That little ventilator on the port side, the after end of the fidley. Near number one stack."

He referred to a galvanized-iron duct that supplied fresh air to the portside passageway on A deck, the writing room on B deck, the passageway on C and finally the foyer on D. When Warms reached it, he saw a trickle of smoke, ran to the officers' quarters to rouse First Officer Ivan Freeman, then hurried back to Hackney.

"Follow up that intake there, Clarence. Look in the passageway on A and then continue down to the writing room. Go all the way to D if you have to and let me know." As an afterthought, as Hackney started down, he added, "Grab that fire extinguisher by the lobby and take it with you."

Daniel Campbell and the butcher from Brooklyn had by now reached the writing room, and though there was smoke in the room, it was coming not from the furnishings or rug but from a locker accessible only to members of the crew. Campbell later recalled, "I opened it, and what I knew once as a locker was one mass of flames, flames from top to bottom and from one side to the other side."

He slammed it shut and ran aft to the deck pantry where he knew the night watchmen were making sandwiches. Arthur Pender and Jerry Dunn were there and he shouted, "We have a fire in the writing room. Go tell the bridge immediately."

He grabbed the phone, got the switchboard, and told the operator, Henry Stamm, "We have a serious fire in the writing room. Get the stewards and the chief steward and everybody out of bed."

By the time he got back to the writing room, Jerry Dunn had informed the bridge of the location of the fire, and Hackney, having emptied the extinguisher on it, was back reporting on its extent. Only three minutes had passed since the first report of the fire at 2:50.

"It's pretty bad," Hackney told Warms. "We better get water on it."

"Break out the hose and I'll get you the men," Warms said. The storm had grown in weight and now in the sprays of sea and rain, coming at him almost horizontally, there was something detestable. He turned to Joseph Welch, the a.b. on duty. "Get forward and arouse the bo'sun and crew. Tell them to get to their fire stations. Hurry."

Warms didn't know it, but the bo'sun was very drunk. He had been drinking Cuban rum until a little after eleven that night and woke up in a daze when Welch slammed into the fo'c'sle. The men dressed and went out on deck without a "foreman" to direct them.

On a ship the first mate and the bo'sun are the two men with the most direct and intimate connection with the deck department. Warms was no longer first mate but captain and, as captain, could not leave the bridge. The deck department was therefore without its first mate and without its bo'sun, who was drunk.

On his way to the wheelhouse, Warms saw Ivan Freeman, whom he had roused on his way from the fidley. At that time he had told Freeman, "Get up. There's a fire on board. Get down and take charge."

Now, three minutes later, Freeman, having seen the fire and rushed to the engine room to tell the engineers to get up pressure on the fire line, was back to suggest to Warms that they turn the ship toward the beach. The ship was heading into the wind.

Louis Fleischman, a quartermaster on the bridge at the time, heard him, and Warms's reply: "We are not going yet, we can hold her. Get down and take charge."

Warms then went to the pilothouse (it was now exactly 2:55 A.M.), called the engine room on the telephone and said, "Is there a fire down there?"

Cadet Engineer William Tripp, a student from M.I.T., who was logging orders from the bridge at the time, handed the phone to the man in charge, Third Engineer Arthur Stamper.

"No," Stamper said, "but a little smoke is coming in."

In the pilothouse with Warms during this telephone conversation was Quartermaster Samuel Hoffman, steering a course of 2°, or almost due north. A few feet behind him was an instrument that looked like a telephone switchboard, the Derby automatic fire-detecting system. It had buttons that flashed red by the action of excessive heat (160° Fahrenheit) on thermostats installed in all the passengers' staterooms, officers' quarters and crew's quarters. Hoffman had already glanced at it, but since public spaces on the ship—like the writing room where the fire was located—were not equipped with the system, he saw no indication of fire on the board.

"Have Abbott call me the moment he gets there," Warms continued over the phone, "and get steam on the main fire pump."

4

Chief Engineer Abbott never did get to the engine room. He had been wakened by the alarm and was at that moment in his quarters putting on a full-dress white uniform.

A fire on a ship calls for work clothes, on engineers especially, and Abbott's taking the time to put on a full-dress uniform was remembered afterwards and given much attention by the newspapers, steamboat inspectors, and Grand Jury. In view of Captain Wilmott's suspicions of sabotage, however, Abbott's desire to be quickly and easily identifiable is perhaps understandable. A man wearing chevrons, gold braid and an officer's cap with "Chief Engineer" written over the peak is not likely to be either lost in the confusion or personally harmed in the presence of witnesses. The breaking out of fire eight hours after the sudden death of Captain Wilmott might have convinced the most stable of men, at least while the alarm was still ringing in his ears, of the truth of the captain's suspicions.

When Abbott finished dressing, he called the engine room from his quarters and got First Engineer Anthony Bujia on the operating platform. Bujia had been asleep in the same quarters with Abbott and aroused by the same alarm; but having dressed less formally (in a one-piece boiler suit), he had left ahead of Abbott and gone directly below.

"How are things down there?" Abbott said.

"Some smoke coming in," Bujia said, "but no flame."

An elevator ran directly down to the engine room from the engineers' quarters on the bridge deck, but Chief Engineer Abbott did not take it because it was full of smoke. He first went down the port companionway to A deck where he saw a large number of men breaking out hose and turning on hydrants. The fire was inside, in the superstructure; and when he saw how negligible the water pressure was, he started shouting, "Open the valve! Open the valve!"

William O'Sullivan, the deck storekeeper ("I was not

taking orders from him") turned and shot back, "The valve *is* open."

It never occurred to Abbott to find out whether any of his men were present. The men themselves, while waiting for the water pressure to become effective, conceived the idea of throwing deck chairs overboard. Without a bo'sun or first mate to direct them (Freeman had gone to report to Warms), a few asked Abbott for permission to throw the chairs.

Abbott then went down to the promenade on B to check, and continued to C, where three very excited women passengers, clutching at his white uniform and the security it symbolized, wanted to know what they should do.

Abbott opened the door to the crew's stairway for them and said, "Go up to the boat deck and wait there." He pointed the way up but did not escort them, then proceeded down to D, two decks above the engine room.

Up to this point, approximately ten minutes having elapsed since he left his quarters, Abbott had done nothing criminal. It was certainly his function to "ascertain the extent of the fire and to see if the hoses were working" before proceeding to the engine room; and though he might be (and was) criticized for not personally escorting the three women to the boat deck, the crew's stairway up which he directed them was not on fire, and it *was* urgent that he get to the engine room.

On D deck he met First Engineer Anthony Bujia, on his way up from the engine room, and the sight of him ascending the steel stairway must not only have shocked Abbott, but robbed him of whatever desire he had left to descend.

"Is that you, Mr. Bujia?"

"Yes."

"What are you doing? Where are you going?"

"To the bridge. I called you through the telephone and speaking tube and got no answer."

"How is everything below?"

"The machinery is fine. Perfect. But smoke is coming in and I don't think the men can stay much longer."

They hesitated, facing each other on the smoky stairway, Abbott on his way down and Bujia on his way up. It was one of those unpredictable moments that change a man's life. For it is not inconceivable that Abbott's future behavior during this fateful night—behavior which he lived to regret—might have been different if he had actually reached the engine room before confronting Bujia. He was on his way down and would almost certainly have continued down if not for this chance meeting. Had he reached the engine room and seen his men in the quiet performance of their duties, he might have remained and even become a source of inspiration to them. The two decks separating him from that possibly ennobling sight were now, however, hopelessly beyond him.

"You go back and stand by," he said. "I'll go to the bridge myself. Keep the men below by all means. Don't let them leave until they have to. If and when you do have to leave, shut the turbines off, shut off the fuel system to the boilers and leave the steam fire pump running."

It all sounded forthright and explicit, and yet, anyone looking at him as he spoke would have detected an extreme reluctance to go below himself. As chief engineer he was responsible for discipline as well as for the operation of the fire pumps, lights and driving power of the ship. But he wanted another look at the fire, to make sure that it wasn't already "every man for himself."

5

By this time the butcher from Brooklyn, Paul Arneth, had gone back to the two couples in the smoking room and said, "The ship's on fire." They had been telling jokes and for a moment thought he was joking. "No, I mean it," Arneth said, and they all got up to look, taking their drinks with them.

There was smoke, all right, but it didn't look as if the officer (Hackney) and the men helping him would have much trouble. The fire was in the ceiling, though, and that was funny because you don't start a ceiling burning with a match or a cigarette. They kept looking; then other late drinkers appeared, staggering up and laughing as though outside a saloon. One man forgot about the brandy he was holding and let it drip through his fingers; another, whose wife thought she should go down and tell their friends, told her not to be silly. A few called out encouragement to the fire fighters, encouragement which the stewards acknowledged with, "Don't worry, we'll put it out easy." But the majority said nothing—until two long flames appeared out of the smoke.

"I'm going down and wake my parents," Doris Wacker of Roselle Park, New Jersey, said to her escort.

"Don't," a steward said. "It's not necessary. You'll only cause panic. We'll put it out easy."

No one had thought to close off either the air ducts into the writing room or the fire-screen door separating the writing room from the lounge, however, and suddenly the fire shot out. Even Watchman O'Connor, who was there fighting the fire, did not know there was a fire door between the writing room and lounge, while Sol Livingston, another watchman present, claimed that he had never received instructions about his fire station or what to do in case of fire.

If Second Officer Clarence Hackney, there also, knew about the fire door, he either forgot about it in the excitement or thought he could control the flames without it. Had fire drills been conducted properly on the

Morro Castle, preventive measures would have become automatic on the part of every member of the crew. Fire drills on the *Morro Castle* were not so conducted; they were slipshod affairs in which only a part of the crew participated.

Hackney may have been able to control the fire without the aid of the fire door had it not been for the unnecessary delay—over six minutes—in getting water on the blaze. The reason for this delay, withheld from the public for twenty-five years, was advanced by Acting Third Officer Howard Hansen.

"A woman passenger fell on the deck, wet from a leaky fire station, sprained her ankle and sued the company for twenty-five thousand dollars about a month before the fire. Captain Wilmott then gave orders to take off the hose, cap the stations, and take away spanner wrenches so that they couldn't be fooled with at drills and start water leaking again. When the fire started [in the writing room] every station nearby was out of commission. Hose had to be brought down double length from the top deck, causing a great delay in getting water on the fire."

When the flames breached the deck and began to climb the stairs, Officer Hackney, black and choking, swung on the tuxedoed men and shouted, "Quit standing around like damn fools. This isn't a fire drill. It's a real fire!"

Everything became confused. A woman, sticking her head out a nearby porthole to see what was the matter, screamed; and the same steward who had told Doris Wacker not to wake her parents was now shouting to the other stewards, "We've got to wake the passengers! We've got to wake the passengers!" People began running below for coats and valuables and to tell their friends, running back on deck to see how the fire fighters were progressing, then running below again for things they had forgotten.

Doris Wacker hurried to cabin 228 to tell her parents, only to be told by her mother, "Your father's looking for you!"

Doris stepped back into the corridor and called, and her father, in a bathrobe, returned. "You two get dressed," Doris said. "I forgot my rings."

Her stateroom was around the corner in the same corridor, so she was back in a minute with her two diamond rings, a suitcase and a life preserver. She helped her parents finish dressing, then in their confusion they all put their preservers on backwards, turning one another around and tying them at the back. Less than three feet away from them, on the door, was a framed-in-glass sign which read in part:

The necessary number of life preservers for adults and children will be found in each stateroom.

Directions for use: Slip the arms through the shoulder straps and secure the belts across the body, under the arms.

Meanwhile, on the navigating deck, Quartermaster Fleischman grabbed a coiled hose and handed it down, with an ax, to the men fighting the fire from the starboard side of A deck. He recognized O'Sullivan, the storekeeper, among them, seamen Thomas and Charles, and Gus Klinger, a junior engineer. They were shouting and throwing deck chairs overboard. This commotion outside cabins one, three and five, plus the seepage of smoke within the superstructure itself, aroused Dr. Cochrane in cabin number one. This was the doctor who, with his sister Catherine and Dr. and Mrs. Vosseler, had been Captain Wilmott's guests that afternoon.

Confused by the sudden awakening, choking and unable to see because of the smoke in the cabin, Cochrane began groping and feeling for the door just as Dr. Vosseler, rushing from the portside to warn him of the fire, started pounding on it. Cochrane, in the nude, handed Vosseler an overcoat to pass to his sister, Catherine, while he slipped his bathrobe on. ("Right next door, cabin number three! Break in her window from the outside if you can't get to the door.")

After Vosseler left, Cochrane, suffocating from the smoke, realized there wasn't time to put on his trousers or his shoes. Wearing only the bathrobe, and in his bare feet, he tried to find the door again. He got down on his hands and knees and felt along the wall, and when he came to the bed he remembered the porthole just above it. This port faced the bow, however, and except for a narrow ledge running athwart the forepart of the super-structure on a level with A deck, the drop to the fore-deck was over twenty feet. And yet this was the port through which fresh air was coming, which made it the likeliest, if not the safest, exit. He got up on the bed, twisted so as to be able to hold on to the edge of the port as he slid down, and lowered himself to the ledge along which he precariously sidled—"the ship was pitching and heaving"—until he reached the starboard rail of A deck where the men were playing a hose. (Dr. Vosseler had disappeared, having been told by a seaman to get his wife forward to the bow. "You'll be safe up there.")

Cochrane thereupon climbed over the rail to A deck, rushed to his sister's window, and said to the men with the hose, "There's a woman in this room!"

O'Sullivan immediately grabbed a hydrant wrench and broke the window. Cochrane was a huge burly man; O'Sullivan was short and slim. There was a moment's hesitation as Ivan Freeman came up; then O'Sullivan said, "I'll go in."

Freeman, lean and muscular, hoisted him by the feet and dumped him in headfirst. The room was so thick with smoke that O'Sullivan's flashlight couldn't penetrate it. He called, "Anybody here?" but received no answer.

He began fumbling around through the beds, which were empty but seemed to have been slept in. Just then he thought he heard something—"it was hard to tell, there was so much noise outside"—and got down on his hands and knees and began feeling around on the floor.

Dr. Cochrane's sister was in her cabin (she perished in it) but this was not her cabin. In his confusion and haste, Cochrane had passed her window and pointed into cabin number five, just aft of his sister's cabin. So that while O'Sullivan was searching for her in number five, she was overcome in her sleep in number three.

"O'Sullivan!" Ivan Freeman began shouting from the deck outside. "O'Sullivan!"

Freeman's impatience saved the storekeeper's life. For he had fallen over a trunk, completely lost his sense of direction, and was just about to pass out when Freeman's cry—the direction from which it came—sent him lunging for the port. They saw his hands and pulled and lifted him out on deck. "I couldn't find her," he said. "There's no one in that cabin."

6

The smoke that had almost overcome O'Sullivan was looked upon by Warms, on the bridge, as a good sign. The boys were dousing the fire, he thought, so there would naturally be a temporary increase in the amount of smoke. When he saw it pour out a door and up the companionway just forward of the writing room, he was relieved.

Just then, like an outrage upon his confidence, the smoke turned to flame and, in the wheelhouse, a button on the electric fire-detecting system turned red, indicating a temperature of 160° Fahrenheit in one of the cabins on A deck. Quartermaster Hoffman had noticed the sudden glare on the portside window of the wheel-house and, glancing automatically round at the board, was about to call out when Warms came in (followed by Quartermaster Fleischman) and saw it himself.

Even under the circumstances that little red light was a stunning thing to see, for not once since the ship was built had a button on the board turned red. Its inoperative existence had been taken so much for granted that now its deadly impartial precision seemed almost unfair —at once unbelievable and demanding of belief.

"A deck, cabin number——" Warms started to say, when suddenly the whole board, indicating intense heat all the way down to C deck, flashed red.

"My God! They're all going."

He pulled the general alarm, rang "Stand by" on the engine-room telegraph, and rushing out to the port wing on the bridge, called in to Hoffman, "Left wheel"—to turn the ship toward the New Jersey shore so that the wind would come in over the starboard quarter and keep the fire blown into the forward portside, the en-closed promenade of B deck, where it was still localized in the writing room.

Warms did not give this left-wheel order until after 3:00 A.M. (using as a guide Cadet Engineer Tripp's 3:00 A.M. logging of the stand-by order in the engine room), which meant that the ship, traveling at 18.8 knots, had already gone 3.1 miles on its northward course against a twenty-knot wind since the first report of the fire at 2:50. A wind, therefore, whose total force was almost forty knots (counting both the speed of the ship and the speed of the wind against it) had been unnecessarily fanning the fire below for over ten minutes.

Groping for his sense of command ("Hard left!"), Warms remembered that on the ship's departure from Cuba, Captain Wilmott had ordered the smoke-detector system turned off. This system, distinct from the electric fire-detecting system, operated by the action of an exhaust fan drawing continuous samples of air from the ship's cargo spaces through pipes to a cabinet in the wheelhouse. It was so effective that the smoking of a cigarette in the hold would have been detected; and, indeed, it was this very effectiveness that had prompted Wilmott to have the air samples emptied outside the wheelhouse on this homeward trip. Number two hold had been filled with wet salty hides during the one-day stopover, and Wilmott had thought the passengers might otherwise complain of the stench. The irony of his trying to keep the customers happy in this case was that they were thereby left without the protection of the smoke-detecting system's most important adjunct—the wheelhouse crew's sense of smell.

On a dark and rainy night when the wheelhouse crew would naturally be using sheltered alleyways and stairways to get to and from their posts, smoke might have been coming through the pipes and discharging into the open air for hours without being seen. The exhaust ducts from number two 'tween decks might have become overheated and set the woodwork adjacent to these ducts afire within the false ceiling in the forward lobby. The steel structure around the funnel might have been red-hot for hours, sending heat along the steel deckbeams, plates and stanchions and charring the wood and wire insulation.

The possibility of sabotage had been advanced by the one man on the ship who now could not be touched by it—the dead captain himself. Wilmott's premonition "that something was going to happen," his threatened dismissal of the radio operator and fear of some vengeful act could no longer be put down to high blood pressure and nervousness. The writing room where the fire originated would have been one of the best possible places to conceal an incendiary device. Like all the public rooms adjoining it, it had no fire-detection apparatus. The locker in the room contained writing materials and over 150 blankets which had been stored there for the summer months. Furthermore, the room had a false ceiling above which was an open space—except for wood furring and steel beams—that ran above the lobby, lounge and smoking-room false ceilings as well. The locker in the writing room communicated directly with all this unseen space, and was itself hidden from view by a door behind which a fire could reach great intensity before being discovered.

Last and most important of all—and withheld from the public for twenty-five years—was the location of the ship's Lyle gun (a line-throwing apparatus).

"The ship's Lyle gun was over the top of the writing room," Acting Third Officer Howard Hansen said. "Warms had a small cabin and the Lyle-gun powder was in his care. It was also in his cabin, so one day he got a large pretzel can, about a five-gallon size, put all the powder (twenty pounds) in it, carried the can to the gun, lashed the can under the barrel of the gun and put the canvas cover over the whole works."

Arson is indicated if a fire reaches great intensity before it is discovered, if it spreads rapidly and in an unusual manner, and if the flames change color when water is applied, indicating the presence of chemicals. In the case of the *Morro Castle* fire all of these elements were in evidence.

"Never before in the history of the merchant service has a fire starting in the locker in a writing room of a ship ended by destroying the ship," William McFee, the noted marine authority, reported afterwards. "If I had read it in a fiction story, I would have said a landlubber wrote it."

"The fire started nowhere else but in that locker,"

Steward Daniel Campbell said, though he, too, was at a loss as to how it could have gained such headway with the door closed and no air to feed it. "The fire could not have been purely accidental. I mean it couldn't have been started by a cigarette or something like that. It spread so fast, the ship might have been made of celluloid. You could not have controlled that fire. I said to Pender, 'I don't think we can save the ship.' The hoses were playing water on the flames, but you might as well have thrown a match in a bucket of water."

Arthur Pender said a "blue-white" flame shot out of the locker, which would indicate a temperature of 1500° Centigrade. "It looked like a chemical fire," he said.

Trygue Johnson, the ship's assistant chief carpenter, had no sooner arrived on the scene and noted the extent of the fire than he too "thought it was set."

"The fire spread very fast and it seemed to go all over at once," Paul Arneth said.

Clarence Hackney, another one of the first men on the scene, made this comment: "I'm positive the fire was set. If a cigarette started it, it might have burned a rug or a drapery, but that's all. That fire must have been inside and burning away for some time."

Not only did the fire appear out of control at the time it was discovered, not only did it spread with unbelievable speed, but the direction of the spread was *downward.*

"I saw fire coming down the stairway from B deck," the ship's cruise director, Robert Smith, said, and several other witnesses bore him out.

"Are you sure?" he was asked. "The fire was racing *downward?*"

"I'm positive. I saw it."

Last but not least is the fact that the flame, when Hackney threw water on it, changed color. Pender saw a blue-white flame. Hackney, throwing water on it, saw a yellow flame. If a flame burns brighter or changes color when water is used, the presence of chemicals is indicated.

Chief Radio Operator Rogers's story that he had thrown a foul-smelling liquid overboard was never corroborated. He said nothing about it until confronted by Wilmott with the knowledge that two bottles had been brought aboard in Havana. He then told Wilmott (according to what Wilmott later told both Warms and Howard Hansen) that he had thrown two bottles overboard.

His claim that there was only one bottle and that it did not contain acid is significant in view of the fact that he was, in addition to being an expert electrician and an experienced mechanic, an amateur chemist. As a youth he completed what was then equivalent to a full course in engineering at the Heel Technical School in San Francisco. He read scientific books and every popular science magazine of the day, and often experimented with delayed-action timing devices, gas-forming combinations and electricity. His knowledge of the reaction between certain acids and compounds was so sure that he had a theory about the Black Tom Explosion which attracted international interest during World War I.

The Black Tom Explosion, according to Rogers, was the result of a fire caused by an incendiary fountain pen clipped to a workman's pocket when his coat was hung up for the night in a closet. Rogers knew how this theoretical fountain pen had been constructed, the ingredients that had gone into it and approximately how long it would have taken for the pen to burst into flame. The cylinder of the pen would have been divided into two sections by a thin membrane of copper, he said. With the pen in a vertical position, the acid in the top section would have eaten through the copper to join the compound in the bottom section. The chemical action thus created would have generated terrific heat and released a large amount of oxygen to cause an intense fire. Experimenting with the thickness of the copper could easily, he said, have guaranteed a delayed action for any period desired.

In this light, Wilmott's "two bottles" become as incriminating as his interpretation of them was naïve. The acid had not been brought aboard to blind or disfigure him, nor had the foul-smelling liquid been a stench bomb.

"What could have been in that locker to turn the ship into a blazing hell in thirty minutes," William McFee wrote afterwards. "One wonders."

In their book *Arson,* published almost twenty years after Rogers's expert description of an incendiary fountain pen (and a more innocent-looking object would have been hard to find in the writing room of a ship), Brendon P. Battle and Paul B. Weston write: "Various chemical combinations have been used to set fires. . . . A unit which provides for an acid to be released upon some combination of chemicals is a favorite device, with the acid releasing itself by eating its way through the cork or even the metal of its container. The time lag from setting to ignition can be estimated with some certainty by an arsonist with a little knowledge of chemistry.

"A chemical combination which can be used to produce a fire is potassium chlorate, sugar, and sulphuric acid. Potassium chlorate is used in various industrial processes such as the manufacture of textiles, medicines, dyes and paper. Table sugar is obtainable anywhere, and sulphuric acid is a well-known and easily obtainable substance."

Rogers's first known attempt to make himself a hero followed an explosion in 1919, involving acid and potassium hydrate. He was an electrician third class in the navy at the time, stationed at the Newport Rhode Island Naval Base.

"One of the seamen was filling a battery," he said. "We had two types of batteries in the radio station at Newport. One was a lead acid battery and one a nickel hydrate battery, and we had a solution of potassium hydrate for the nickel hydrate batteries and an acid solution for the acid batteries. The potassium hydrate was practically colorless; you could hardly distinguish it from plain water. And this seaman drew a beaker of what he thought was water out of the potassium acid and had put it in the battery and I happened to notice that the thing he was working on was painted red, which signified it wasn't water, and I rushed at him. I didn't want to frighten him by calling, so I rushed at him and the acid struck me in the eyes and I couldn't tell you whether it was really an explosion or just a violent chemical action. The reaction of the intense hydrate and the intense acid would be to separate violently, and I got it in the eyes, and I was taken right to the Naval Hospital and I was unconscious for quite a while, and they told me I was delirious with pain and burn. I was discharged later on, got a discharge not recommended for re-enlistment."

This story does not tally with Rogers's navy record, which states that on January 24, 1920, he was brought

before a Board of Medical Survey, and his case diag-
nosed as amblyopia (dimness of vision without detect-
able organic lesion of the eye). He was found permanently unfit for service and the board recommended his
discharge from the navy. Rogers had entered the Naval
Hospital on December eighth with some sort of burn,
but the Survey Board, obviously disagreeing as to what
had happened with the acid and potassium hydrate,
considered "the degree of disability in his case to be
zero %, because of the fact that the condition existed at
the time of his enlistment."

Though fire investigation has made great advances
in the last twenty-five years, an arsonist is still one of
the most difficult criminals to convict. "In no other
crime does circumstantial evidence play such an important part as it does in arson," Messrs. Battle and Weston
write. "Direct evidence is almost impossible to obtain.
Very few people ever see someone set a fire."

The pathological firesetter, however, unless appre-
hended and convicted in time, usually sets more than
one fire. Indeed, since the irresistible impulse which
leads to his setting the first fire usually returns after a
psychic fallow period, his presence at more than one
suspicious fire is often a fire investigator's only lead.
George W. Rogers "was present on several occasions at
fires of a suspicious nature," according to records on
file at the New Jersey State Penitentiary in Trenton.

These fires both preceded and followed the *Morro Castle* fire, and, like the latter, are still unsolved.

On the morning of September 21, 1929, for example, a mysterious fire broke out at 179 Greenwich Street in New York City. The night man, who had a set of keys, locked the building at 11:30 P.M. and left. George W. Rogers, a mechanic employed in the building by the Wireless Egert Company, had another set of keys. Rogers usually arrived for work and opened the building at 8:30 A.M. On the morning of the fire he was at the scene at 7:30. When the firemen arrived at 7:45, Rogers unlocked the building and let the firemen in. The fire is still unsolved and a report of it, on file in the Fire Marshal's office in New York in 1934, is, thirty years after the fire, still on file.

A year after the *Morro Castle* fire, another mysterious fire broke out in Rogers's own radio repair shop in Bayonne, New Jersey. Rogers collected $1,175 in insurance, but later, according to the same prison report, "he was found to have set this fire with a soldering iron wrapped with matches, and to have used a blow torch to destroy further property in his shop."

Further substantiating the theory of incendiarism on the *Morro Castle* is the fact that the writing room *ceiling* had been afire when Hackney arrived on the scene. This meant that the chemically intense fire in the locker itself, as observed two or three minutes earlier by Pender and Campbell, had not been limited to the locker but had already spread unseen and unobstructed to the wood furring behind the false ceiling, above which was stored twenty pounds of black gunpowder in a five-gallon pretzel can.

The almost head-on wind, therefore, seeping through the flush forepart of the superstructure, might have been feeding an unseen, willfully set fire for hours, long before the butcher from Brooklyn had said he smelled smoke. Indeed, it is not unreasonable to suppose that shortly after midnight, when Una Cullen and Mae Maloney and their two gentlemen friends first entered the smoking room with their Havana-bought rum, the fire, originating in the writing-room locker, had already worked its way aft above the false ceilings and was burning above them when they clinked glasses in mutual congratulation of a successful trip.

A kind of listless sorrow came over Warms. Not only had Wilmott's death had a profound effect on him, but a fire that may have been set, and must, in any case, have reached 1500° in that locker before it was ever discovered, was now threatening the ship itself. The very sequence of events since the ship's departure from Havana seemed to preclude the element of chance.

Further, the idea of a ship's burning under his command had haunted Warms for years, ever since a ten-day suspension in 1926 by the Steamboat Board for not holding fire and boat drills as master of the *Yumuri,* a Ward Line freighter. That suspension had made him a stickler for fire and boat drills ever since, but who would believe that now?

How many times had he gone to the glory hole on this ship and kicked in the doors of stewards failing to attend fire and boat drills? How many times had he asked Wilmott to log them? The idea of simply having the fore gang forward and the after gang aft during fire drills had not been conceived by him but by Wilmott. And when he'd asked Wilmott, "How about these men going to their fire stations, to all the hydrants, and stringing out hoses?" Wilmott had said, "No, I don't want the men to run around and excite passengers. We have an old sea tradition: 'Excitement brings panic.' I don't want any excitement; it's much better to have a gang forward and a gang aft. If you had a fire forward and you had the men at their stations, they wouldn't go to their stations, they would go to where the fire was."

The ship's cruise director, Robert Smith, corroborated Warms by saying that Captain Wilmott had rejected the suggestion that passengers take part in boat drills. "It might cause undue anxiety among them," Smith quoted Wilmott as saying. "You're safer here than crossing Times Square or South Street."

Commodore Jones, relieving Wilmott one trip, had said essentially the same thing when Warms brought up the question of fire drills. "Yes, those men going to their stations, running all over the ship, would only create excitement."

But no one would believe now that he, Warms, had argued for stiffer fire drills. People would say that that 1926 suspension should have been permanent.

Such was the momentary lapse of a weary man in the throes of discovering his naked identity—a man who had had his rightful authority as chief officer on the ship weakened and undermined but who now, suddenly and in the greatest of all crises that can befall a captain at sea, held complete and absolute authority. A demand as disproportionate as it was unforeseen was about to be made on his last reserves of strength, and he was determined to meet it. There was in fact nothing inactive about him; no one in the grip and clamor of the moment noticed anything wrong. With his captain enviably dead, he had the courage and imagination to experience an anxiety based in reality, which is vastly different from being a coward.

Fire at Sea

7

It was just before 3:00 A.M., not quite ten minutes after
the discovery of the fire, when Third Radio Operator
Charles Maki rushed into the radio operators' quarters
to arouse Rogers and Alagna.

"As I opened the door the alarm went off," he said.

Alagna was already awake, having heard the shouting and tramping of feet outside. "What next?" he
thought aloud, remembering Captain Wilmott's sudden
death. Grabbing a pair of trousers, he jumped down
from his bunk, below which Maki slept, and started
dressing.

Rogers, across the cabin in a single bed, did not stir until after the alarm sounded. Both Alagna and Maki witnessed this fact, and Alagna said he remembered having "to shake him quite hard to wake him." Rogers, therefore, had two eyewitnesses to prove that he had been asleep when the fire started, and on another deck from where it originated.

"Pyromaniacs usually make elaborate plans for their fires, establish alibis for themselves and generally are not at the scene of the fire," Fritz Byloff writes in his study of pyromania. "On the other hand they are drawn to the fire, having a hunger to see the excitement and to rid themselves of an unendurable psychic sensation."

"Get back to your post," Rogers said to Maki. "I'll be right there."

Alagna reached the radio room ahead of Rogers, at exactly 3:00 A.M. He was certain of the time because he had the four-to-eight watch and made note that he had "an hour to go." On his way from his sleeping quarters he saw flames "so great that they led me to believe the fire had been raging for at least an hour before I was awakened."

This was doubtful, as evidenced by a 2:50 A.M. entry in the radio log by Charles Maki. At that time, only ten minutes before Alagna saw a raging fire, Maki saw no fire at all. What Maki did see was smoke, and within the radio room itself. It was curling up from behind a wastebasket under his desk, seemingly sourceless, since there was no evidence of fire either inside or outside the room.

"It came from behind a wastebasket on the portside of the radio room. I entered the fact in the log."

The radio room was made of steel and had a fireproof Selbalith flooring laid on top of steel. The smoke could not have seeped through the steel or Selbalith, and if it had come through the door or port, it would not have remained invisible until it began curling upward from behind the wastebasket. The smoke that Maki observed must have originated in the radio room, and from something capable of creating smoke without necessarily creating flame. A few remaining drops of sulphuric acid, eating through an empty bottle's cork and dropping on a wet rag or a scrap of paper, would have created a small trickle of smoke such as Maki observed.

Rogers had the radio-room watch immediately preceding Maki's. The captain's death had by then created a climate of confusion in which suspicious things would go unnoticed or, if noticed, unreported. It was during this last of Rogers's scheduled watches in the radio room, for example, that Night Watchman Arthur Pender, passing by on his rounds at 10:30, became aware of a strong odor of gasoline. "I did not report it to the bridge because I put it down to late cleaning on the eve of the ship's arrival in port," he said.

That he should associate a smell of gasoline with the steward's department and for that reason not report it to the bridge is in itself revealing of the state of affairs on the *Morro Castle* that night. Much more important is the fact that if he had reported a smell of gasoline less than three hours after the captain's sudden and mysterious death, the entire ship might have been alerted.

There were two gasoline tanks, feeding a motor attached to the radio-sending apparatus, outside the radio room. Rogers was on watch only a few feet from these tanks when and where Pender smelled gasoline. It was definitely established that the feed line from these tanks to the motor had been uncoupled before the fire started, leaving nothing but vacuum to hold the gasoline in the tanks, because the parts later oxidized separately, which would not otherwise have been the case. When Pender made his rounds at 10:30, the feed line must have been uncoupled and already giving off an odor. Furthermore, the uncoupling would have to have been accomplished with a wrench and could not have been an accident.

A man with wrenches at his disposal, on duty less than fifteen feet away from this feed line, who knew that the night watchman would not be back on his rounds until 10:30 and that most of the ship's officers were in the dead captain's quarters, could have stepped out on deck, uncoupled the feed line to spread a fire that he knew would soon be starting, and returned to his post in less than a minute. As the tanks became heated from the fire originating below, the gas would expand, pass out through the feed line, and contaminate the decks, stairways and cabins in that vicinity. This explains the fire's strange "downward" spread and also Arthur Pender's statement that two of the cabins below these tanks burst into solid sheets of flame very early in the fire.

"An incendiary mechanism may be mechanical or chemical," write Battle and Weston. "It consists of an ignition device, possibly a timing mechanism, one or more 'plants' to feed or accelerate the initial flame, and frequently 'trailers' to spread the fires."

A five-gallon pretzel can containing twenty pounds of black gunpowder almost directly above the writing room was a ready-made "plant." That still others were used is evidenced by Pender's statement that he saw "three separate fires burning simultaneously" and by Alagna's describing a ten-minute fire as one that must have been raging for at least an hour. The use of a "trailer" is conclusively proven by the fact that the feed line from the gas tanks had been uncoupled before the fire started.

Every possible indication of incendiarism was present. The fire had reached great intensity before it was discovered. It spread with unbelievable speed. The direction of the spread was downward, and there were both "plants" and "trailers." Finally, there was a man aboard who was both morally insane and conversant with incendiary devices, and whose presence at fires of a suspicious nature had been, and was again to be, reported.

Between the first radiogram at 9:30, therefore ("Wilmott deceased at 7:45 P.M. Acknowledge"), and the second at 10:30 P.M. ("Confirming message from Warms," etc.), the dead captain's cremation may have been both planned and assured.

"I can never be convinced that Captain Wilmott died of heart disease due to acute indigestion," Mrs. Wilmott said. "There is something strange about it all."

At 3:01 ship's time (the general alarm was still ringing), Rogers was topside "to assume command of the radio room." The ship was laboring in the storm; there was a heavy ground swell and as she heaved and rolled her glistening rain-wet decks reflected the fire like huge mirrors. "It seemed to be just below and forward on the portside by the writing room," he said. Men fighting it were shouting to one another but the wind carried the commotion, and even the danger, it seemed, out to sea. "It was strange, the sense it gave me after being so soundly asleep, like straddling two ships in a dream, or like being two different people."

And yet he could hear a drumming slosh of water from a hose, and a dense black smoke was rolling off to leeward. The fact was that the whole ship had a hum to it now, and he remembered that over half the passengers were seasick and that there had been several drunken parties in staterooms and cabins throughout the ship. Several couples, festive despite the calling off of the farewell ball after Captain Wilmott's death, had planned parties of their own, with the result that six girls had had to be carried to their rooms by stewards.

The exactitude of Rogers's observation concerning what happened in the radio room between his entering and leaving was looked upon with awe and admiration by those investigating the fire, and since nothing was known of his criminal record, psychiatrists were not consulted.

"I was in complete control of myself and I saw the situation clearly," he recalled twenty-two years later, during an interview in the New Jersey State Penitentiary, where he was serving a life term for the double murder of an old man and his spinster daughter. "I knew what I had to do and why. The excitement was there, inside but hidden. I wasn't even sweating. I was quite calm, in fact. I didn't deliberately make a note of what was happening, but I saw everything happen very clearly. I remember I was grateful for this at the time, because the fire was spreading and someone had to have his wits about him."

In the radio room just before Rogers's arrival, Alagna

noticed that the emergency lamp, required by law to be lighted at all times, was not burning. When he tried another bulb, it still failed to light, which meant that the system was dead.

He informed Rogers of this on the latter's arrival a moment later, and Rogers, telling Maki, "Get out of my way," nodded. Of course at that time the engine-room supply of electrical power was still reaching the radio room, but very significant is the fact that Rogers, the chief operator whose responsibility it was to have the emergency-power failure traced (since the radio would need it if anything happened to the engine-room power), did not order Alagna or Maki to trace it. If he had ordered them to do so, they might have discovered the uncoupled feed line from the gas tanks to the motor feeding the emergency system.

Rogers knew, however, that even if all the electrical power on the ship failed, he would still have a two-battery set in the radio room for sending an S O S. He was determined to send an S O S if necessary, and that auxiliary transmitter was his ace in the hole, since it was controlled independently of everything else by the two batteries in the radio room.

"I then called Rogers's attention to the smoke," Alagna said, "and he came over to a closet and took out a sailing chair, a mattress and a few other things, including some combustible polish. He took that out also."

Captain Wilmott had added to the friction between the radio room and bridge by ordering the assistant radio operators to polish brass when they had nothing else to do. This had become a standing order on the *Morro Castle,* and the radio operators, resenting it as an affront to their real function as officers on the ship, resented even more the ineffectiveness of the paste polish with which they were supplied. "You'll save yourself a lot of elbow grease," a former radio operator named McPherson had told Alagna before signing off the ship himself, "if you mix this paste with kerosene," whereupon he had shown Alagna where the kerosene was stored.

"One of the objects of the strike [in July] was to force the line to limit the operators' work to the radio and free them from serving as 'general flunkies,' " Alagna said.

After helping Rogers and Maki to remove the mattress, sailing chair and polish, Alagna said, "I'll take a look on deck."

The fire had grown, but the lifeboats, he noticed, were still on their chocks on deck. "I saw one man, who I assumed was a passenger, with his arm around the waist of a woman, and the remainder of the group of people there were men, mostly in the striped pants of the steward's department. It impressed me that there they stood, waiting, waiting."

When he returned to the radio room, Rogers said, "George, go to the bridge and see what orders the mate [Acting Captain Warms] has to give."

There is a distinct law among radiomen on ships that calls for the chief operator to take over in an emergency, and for the second operator to act as liaison between the bridge and radio room. The purpose of this is to supplement the regular connections in the event they fail. On the *Morro Castle* these regular connections consisted of a speaking tube, a telephone, and a push button to the switchboard down on D deck.

As Alagna left and Rogers sat down to adjust the transmitter to distress frequency, the ship seemed to turn and a heavy black smoke began coming in. "Maki, wet a towel and give it to me," the chief operator said without looking up.

Rogers was a blubbery man with a huge bathrobe of a body and a well-insulated nervous system. Physically sluggish, his eyes nevertheless showed a keen awareness of what he was doing and why. He seemed utterly incapable of heroics, and perhaps for that reason was to become the disaster's great hero.

Meanwhile, three decks below Rogers, in stateroom 221 on C deck, a young Harvard graduate, Gouverneur Morris Phelps, Jr., had just opened his eyes and was jumping up thinking he had dropped a cigarette before falling asleep and started the fire himself. There was no fire in the room, though, only smoke, and when he opened the door and looked down the corridor, he saw it all aglow with a bright orange flame and dense with smoke.

He pulled back in and shook his roommate, Ed Kendall, who nodded and smiled and then went back to sleep again.

"The ship's on fire!" cried Phelps, yanking the covers off and pulling him bodily out of bed. "Get dressed!"

Then he stuck his head out the porthole and the blood began pounding through his body. "There was a perfect inferno the whole length of the ship," he said later, "great sheets of it leaping high above the lifeboat level."

He and Kendall ran through the corridor and tore a line of hose from the wall, just as John Kempf, a New York City fireman, sharing stateroom 208 on the same deck with a jockey from Worcester, Massachusetts, rushed into the corridor buckling his belt. He had had trouble finding his shoes and the ninety-five pound jockey had sprung from bed and landed right on top of him in the smoky room. The jockey had left in pajamas, but Kempf had stayed to tie his shoes and to pull on a pair of trousers.

"Hey there, big fellow," Phelps called from the other end of the corridor, "you can turn on that valve."

Before opening the valve, Kempf ran the kinks out

of the hose. He assumed the two were ship's officers and could not understand their inexperience, but he kept these thoughts to himself. "I had read articles about ship sinkings," he said later, "and how the officers had flashed their guns, so naturally I worked silently. You see, that is the way my trend of mind ran at the time. I thought one little rug was on fire. We'd roll it up and throw it overboard. I was really thinking of saving my luggage and everything."

When he opened the valve, a vooming, vibrating thunder, as of the ocean itself, ran through, whereupon Phelps and Kendall, tensing up on the nozzle, directed the stream on the elevator door. Smoke was pouring from the elevator shaft and through crevices and other openings in the partitions and woodwork, and though the hose had tremendous pressure, they were playing the water not on fire but on smoke. Phelps and Kendall didn't know it, but the fire was above them, with the smoke pouring down, not up, the elevator shaft.

Kempf didn't know it either, but being an experienced fireman, he realized at a glance that it was no good fighting the fire this way. In fact, as soon as he saw that Phelps and Kendall didn't have guns, he began ordering them around.

"Naturally water isn't effective unless it hits the seat of the fire or the body of the fire," he said later. "That is the way my trend of mind worked. I know nothing about shipbuilding, and in order to extinguish fires effectively you must know construction. I had been on the ship only three days [he had boarded in Havana] and it was always confusing to me; I was not fully acquainted with it."

Phelps and Kendall finally turned the stream on the stairway, sort of trying to blow their way out, all the while yelling, "Fire! Fire!" in an effort to rouse other passengers. All three of them, Phelps, Kendall and Kempf, banged on stateroom doors behind which snores could be heard, desperate scramblings for belongings, cries of "What is it?", and even annoyed matter-of-fact curses as though even death were going to be a nuisance.

Behind one door a man was saying, "Just try—to get me on another ship! From now on I'll meet you there." He must have been seasick because it was all garbled and interrupted by retching, and immediately afterwards came a woman's harassed voice, "Joe, hurry! We'll be trapped here!"

The water in the corridor washed back and forth with the ship's roll, rising two feet in some quarters as it sloshed around. There was plenty of it, but Kempf knew that they were wasting their efforts in this corridor. "You must get to the bottom of a fire to put it out, and besides, no one was cutting off the draft to smother it."

The heat got worse and the smoke rolled down on

them and made them squeeze their eyes against it. It had a peculiar biting quality, and Phelps said later that he knew he would recognize it if he ever encountered it again.

The heady pungency of which he spoke came from the laminated paneling between staterooms, from the glue used in pressing the plywood together and from the stain and varnish applied to bring out the beauty of the wood. Such paper-thin wood, sandwiched perhaps six times over with layers of glue and then coated on the outside with highly inflammable varnish, would not only give off a cutting smoke such as Phelps described, but would also, with the speed of a struck match, add to the intensity of a fire.

They abandoned the hose. Kempf closed down on the valve to keep the pressure up on others, then rushed up to B deck to pound on more doors and to close off drafts wherever possible. ("Naturally, my trend of mind ran always expecting officers with guns.")

Phelps, meanwhile, had left Kendall and raced round to the other corridor on C deck to wake his mother and father in 209. He pounded with both fists on the door and called, "Mother! Father!"

They came out already dressed, the smoke having wakened them, too. Mrs. Phelps had been sleeping in the outer bed next to the porthole, and just two minutes before had said to her husband, a prominent surgeon,

"Gouv, the ship must be afire; smoke is pouring in." They had gone to bed much earlier but had had a hard time getting to sleep because of the noise of people in the corridors going from one party to another. Dr. Phelps knew the time, 3:01 A.M., because his watch had been lying on the dressing table. It was a valuable watch and he had already put it in his pocket.

Now they were both astounded to see their son soaking wet: his hair, clothes, shoes, everything, as though he'd been washed overboard and fished back again. "I've been using a hose," he said. "For heaven's sake, hurry. It's serious."

They could hear the fire crackling as they spoke but were not bewildered. They took hold at once and there came over Dr. Phelps's face a certain stringency of expression, as though serious thought now might bring about the right behavior later. He and his wife went back for money and preservers (there was only one) and came right out again. The three of them tried to go up the companionway to the boat deck, but couldn't because of the smoke. So they started through the corridor toward the stern, meanwhile pounding and hammering on doors to get other sleepers up.

At the stern, crowds were forming. Men came by dragging burned friends or wives whose cries, young Phelps said later, "went straight to the hearts of all who heard them." The fire must have broken into many cabins without warning and caught scores of passengers in their sleep. A man came up to Dr. Phelps and said a boy was badly burned. The boy, one of the Saenz children from Cuba, had been pulled out of a burning cabin by William Derringh, a waiter who with the help of another waiter, Malcolm Ferguson, had carried the boy aft. "His flesh came off on my hand when I picked him up," Ferguson said. "And all during the time we carried him, from A deck to B deck and then down to C, he said just two words, 'Mi madre! Mi madre!'"

There was nothing Dr. Phelps could do: "When I got to him he cried, 'Don't touch me!' and just then the lights went out. . . . Nothing could be done in the darkness, and my wife and son being my first duty, I went back to them at the rail."

The boy died a few minutes later and the two waiters laid the body in a corner out of the way of the rushing crowd.

People were moaning and whimpering and you could hear others praying; and among them stood a tall man in a white uniform with gold stripes and braid, the cruise director, Robert Smith, shouting, "Silence, please. I am waiting for orders from the bridge."

Meanwhile, within the superstructure on other decks, stewards were running and stopping, running and stopping. Each door got a pound and the abrupt admonition, "Bring your preserver and get on deck! Bring your preserver and get on deck!"

Other stewards, on Captain Warms's orders, were actually banging pots and pans through the corridors in an effort to arouse the heavy drinkers who had passed out behind locked doors. One musician in the brass section of the ship's orchestra soon came to their aid by blowing an impromptu reveille through the smoke-filled corridors and stairways.

"When the alarm was sounded," Benjamin Hirsch of Philadelphia said, "there was a banging on tin pans and whistles and bugles were blowing. My wife got her lifebelt on wrong, but I fixed it and then put on my own. We ran out into the corridor. It was as hot as a furnace and I pushed my wife ahead of me toward the stairs. On the deck, men and women were running from one side of the ship to the other. A member of the crew stopped me as I pushed Mrs. Hirsch over toward a lifeboat. 'Give me that preserver, I'm going to give it to a woman,' the seaman said. I didn't believe him, but he took my belt and ran."

The stewards and the man with the trumpet didn't know it, but the switchboard operator down on D deck, Henry Stamm, was helping them in their efforts by plugging in the passengers' quarters about three cabins at a time. After Daniel Campbell's telephone report of the fire from the pantry on B deck, Stamm had called the stewards, mates and engineers and was now working through the passenger list. He started with cabin number one (Dr. Cochrane had already climbed out the port) and worked his way down the switchboard to the 200 section, getting a response about every third time. But then the board went dead, so he left it and went to the rooms in the 300 section to see whether the passengers had been aroused. He found several dressing, woke others, and finally started up the crew's stairway, where he met a priest, Father Egan of St. Mary's Roman Catholic Church in the Bronx, who wanted some member of the crew with an intimate knowledge of the ship to help him reach passengers who were beyond help but still alive.

Father Egan, ordained only fourteen months, was twenty-seven years old, just a little older than Henry Stamm, himself a Catholic. They started off together, through a superstructure that had become a wilderness of motive, desire and intention. Women, half-dressed, scurried through corridors, their husbands helping them, pulling them, clearing ways for them, and all the while holding back their own fear.

In some cases modesty proved fatal, for there was not always time for a woman to slip into a dress, much less to choose one. With the men it was more pride than modesty. One among them, for example, barefoot and naked except for his bathrobe, had got his foot caught between the iron rung of an escape ladder and the bulk-head behind it, but he wasn't saying anything. He had left his false teeth in a glass of water back in his cabin and was too embarrassed to ask for help. People later recalled having looked at him in passing, bewildered themselves, but still finding time to be a little bewildered by him. It was very human and very pathetic to see this attempt at nonchalance while his injured ankle, swelling, locked his foot more and more permanently behind the ladder rung.

Further forward in the same corridor, an old and gentle woman was making a kind of shawl of her bewilderment. She kept considering others and expecting them to consider her, and perhaps for that reason, was considered. People in the most dire straits themselves, choking or looking for some loved one, would notice her almost charming incomprehension of the danger she was in and say something like, "Help this lady somebody! I've got to find my little girl!"

Around in another corridor, otherwise empty, two men going in opposite directions couldn't seem to get past each other. One was trying to get aft away from the fire, the other was trying to get back to his cabin to save his wife. They ducked and swayed and stepped from left to right as though locked in a closet of identical impulse. It began to appear as if there were something personal in the scuffle; the man going aft could not more effectively have prevented the other from saving his wife if he had wanted her to die. And yet he kept shouting, "Get out of my way!"

"Look out, my wife is trapped!" the other man, who had wrapped himself in a wet blanket, kept repeating, "Look out!"

The truth must have been, as the passenger going aft later suggested, that the man was temporarily diverted from his determination to save his wife. The sight of the flames between him and her must have filled his soul with dread, whereupon this pedestrian mishap had occurred, during which he stepped every way but forward. He actually began clinging to the man going aft, grabbing his jacket, until he found himself sitting in the corridor with a bloody nose. From the after end of the corridor, the other man, who asked that his name be withheld, saw him get up and, with his arms covering his face, run into the flames from which he never returned. (The remains of a man's body was found in this corridor several days later by Robert W. Hodge of the U. S. Coast Guard.)

Every yard of corridor contained a drama of its own, while behind many locked doors, sleep and drowsiness, seasickness and intoxication, clung to people's minds and limbs like the devil's own gossamer. One man was so drunk that he almost lost himself between the possibility of saving his life and the natural instinct to do so.

He had passed out an hour before and been put to bed by a friend, in the friend's room. And now all his hazy mind could grasp, he said afterward, as the steward shouted through the door, "Get dressed, Mr. Brady. The ship's on fire! Bring your preserver," was that he wasn't Brady. The thought occurred to him, as he fell back into a drunken sleep: Muz remember—tell Brady. Mustn't forget.

Luckily, Brady, who later drowned, came back in time to rouse him.

8

Out on the weather side of the bridge, Captain Warms could not focus his eyes on Alagna, much less listen to him. The gale was whirring against the ship, supplying all the oxygen the fire needed, and he was shouting at the top of his lungs to the deck hands below on A deck, "Don't break those windows!"

Didn't they realize that breaking them would make flues of the very corridors the passengers were escaping through? He brushed Alagna aside and shouted until his very lungs pained from the effort. "Don't—break—those—windows! Close all doors—on this—side!"

But the wind unmercifully censored him, and the men, hearing or thinking they heard, not orders but cries for help, went on breaking windows and opening doors so as not to trap people trying to get through them to the boats. And though they played tons of water into the openings they made, the gale found the fire first and sent it racing everywhere.

This tragedy was repeated all over the ship. Shouted orders full of urgency and good sense were given no better treatment by the wind than the hysterical cries of women. Indeed, it was hard in the tumult to distinguish between an authoritative voice, necessarily straining itself to be heard, and one pleading for instructions from someone in authority. "Help those passengers to get to the boats," became indistinguishable from just plain "Help!" No one knew to whom to listen or where to go, so that the captain, from whose vantage point everything could be seen—the confusion, the growth of the fire, the helplessness of seasick passengers and the bungling of an uninstructed crew—felt that his very brain was turning on a skewer.

"Captain, what about—— Are there any instructions?" Alagna began, cursing himself for not wearing his radio officer's cap. Didn't Warms even know who he was?

What Alagna didn't know was that Captain Wilmott had suspected him of trying to sabotage the ship and that perhaps Warms, pursued as much by Wilmott's suspicions as by Alagna himself (hadn't he suggested locking Alagna up?), did not *want* to listen to him.

Warms pushed him away and stood seething with fury and frustration as the ship, as if persisting in being a ship to the very end, started on a series of rolls and the seamen on A deck began playing one leg against the other in an effort to hold their balance. It was obvious that they hadn't heard him, and their flame-lit movements, the hair flying straight off from their scalps, the pugnacity of wind against their trousered legs, were things that Warms would never forget as long as he lived. There was an unbearable poignancy in the sight of them that he would always associate with the loss of the ship, and with his one abortive day as master of it.

It was at this moment that Alagna made a most un-usual request: "Captain, what about Wilmott's body? Can I put it in one of the boats?"

This suggestion from Alagna detained Warms for a moment, for if there was anything suspicious about Wilmott's death, why would the man most likely to be suspected of murdering him want to preserve the evidence? If Wilmott's body were left aboard and cremated, almost any unprovable charge could be made against Alagna. Did he know he was suspected of sabotage and already foresee his arrest? If so, he must have realized what an important part an autopsy of Wilmott's body would play in the proceedings.

But Clarence Hackney had rushed to the bridge, over-heard Alagna's suggestion, and, after telling Warms, "I can't control it!", turned to Alagna and said, "The living are more important than the dead."

"Lower the boats to the rail," Warms said to Hackney and, as Hackney left, ran to the starboard wing of the bridge. "My God [the hoses were turning to syringes in the men's hands], what's happened to the water pres-sure?"

He shoved Alagna out of the way and started on the run in search of Chief Engineer Abbott—with Alagna right behind.

"Abbott! Where are you?" Warms shouted, ignoring Alagna's attempts to get through to him. "Chief—God damn it, where *are* you?"

They found Abbott hunched in a secure place outside the wheelhouse on the weather side, where the wind would naturally protect him from the fire—a limp wit-ness of the fact that others were still trying. He was wringing his hands and crying, "What are we going to do? What are we going to do?"

Alagna had been struck by the sight of him before be-cause Abbott had no business on the bridge, and by the fact that he was all dressed up in full uniform as though he were going to the captain's ball. He was coughing and looked a little decomposed already, shorter and smaller than he was because all tension was gone from his spine, the middle vertebrae of which were against the wheelhouse.

"What's happened to the water pressure?" Warms shouted at him.

"It's too late——" Abbott began. "Hundred hoses couldn't hold this fire now."

Abbott, who had been consulted throughout the *Morro Castle's* construction in 1930 at Newport News, knew that the steam fire pump at 100 pounds pressure had a capacity of 1000 gallons a minute, and that the 2 electric sanitary pumps added another 300 gallons a minute to the ship's fire-fighting capacity. He knew also that all 3 pumps discharged water into the same main and that though there were 42 hydrants situated throughout the ship, only 6 could be supplied with full pressure (30 pounds at each nozzle) at any one given time. With 12 hydrants open, the pressure at each nozzle would drop to at least one third of normal.

Now John Kempf, the New York City fireman, and young Phelps and Kendall, the two Harvard boys, were not the only passengers to use hoses in the corridors below. Several others, in different corridors and on different decks, had done the same thing, only unlike John Kempf, who naturally realized the importance of turning a hydrant off before abandoning it, these passengers had dropped the nozzles of their hoses and run for their lives. These hoses were thereupon burned off the hydrants, which meant that the wide-open valves, devoid of even the smaller nozzle openings to slow down the flow of water, were releasing pressure (ineffectually) as fast as the pumps could supply it. To make matters worse, these abandoned hydrants were closer to the source of supply, in both a distance and a gravity sense, than the hydrants on the higher decks to which Warms referred, so that while the unmanned hydrants were being supplied with water, the manned hydrants were being robbed of it.

All Abbott would have had to do to prevent this tragedy of a growing fire with less and less water to fight it (it was too late now, but he had been doing absolutely nothing for twenty minutes) was go down through the superstructure, or delegate one of his men to go down (and his men were all about, uninstructed by any superior) and turn the other hydrants off.

"Answer me!" Warms shouted at him. "What's happened to it?" But before Abbott could answer, the man at the wheel sang out, "Captain, she's not holding!" and Warms, more interested in hearing what a man still doing his duty had to say, ran into the wheelhouse to find Quartermaster Hoffman flying the wheel around as though it were attached to his own failing brain.

Hoffman had swung the wheel hard over in response to Warms's "Hard left," and though the ship had responded (the course now was almost due west—273 degrees), the gyrocompass, electrically controlled, and the electric steering apparatus, seemed to have burned out.

"She's not holding, sir," Hoffman said.

"Try the magnetic. Hard left."

Warms wanted the stern of the ship to the wind so the smoke and flame would be blown forward, away from the passengers who had found refuge aft. The ship, however, was now broadside to the wind, with all her windward glass broken, thus allowing an endless supply of oxygen into lobbies veneered with mahogany and rosewood and extending through four decks.

These lobbies, one forward and one aft, and each with a hardwood stairway built around an elevator shaft, communicated directly with the two main passageways on each deck, so that if the wind, as the ship swung, stopped feeding the fire from one direction, it immediately started feeding it from another. To confine such a fire as the present one, there were steel bulkheads fitted with sliding steel doors not more than 13 feet apart on each passenger deck, but these had not been closed at the first report of the fire at 2:50, and were not closed now for fear of trapping passengers trying to escape. Indeed, as the fire grew, and things that might have been done were not done, as one effort canceled out another and ignorance succeeded where negligence failed, the ship itself, from other shipping lanes, appeared out of control or piloted by madmen.

"Swing her as far as she'll go," Warms was saying. "Turn her south, one hundred and eighty degrees."

But when Hoffman swung the magnetic-compass wheel, operated hydraulically, it remained slack, which meant that the oil was not being put under pressure. He turned it to the right, then to the left again, and it still remained slack, which meant that the ship, still broadside to the wind, now had a powerless rudder.

The only thing left for Warms to do was to back and fill on the engines, that is, go ahead on one, astern on the other, and keep the ship's stern to the wind that way. This meant running out to the wing of the bridge to see how fast the stern was swinging, calling in to Hoffman for a compass reading, running in and reversing the engines again in the event the stern started either way too far, and running out again to direct the men fighting the fire and to delegate other men to help passengers into the boats.

Meanwhile, Ivan Freeman had returned to the bridge, black and coughing, to report the fire out of control. In the darkness and smoke he brushed against Quartermaster Fleischman and said, "Wasn't Warms in a position to see the full extent of the fire?"

Just then Warms, rushing out of the wheelhouse, saw Freeman and cried, "For God's sake, get forward and prepare to let go the anchor. We have a powerless ship!"

They both started on the run, Freeman toward the

bow, Warms after Abbott, with Alagna, still trying desperately to get orders to send an S O S, right behind.

"Too late——" Abbott kept saying, "Too late. Hundred hoses . . ."

Warms appeared on the verge of becoming someone else: that the fire *was* out of control had fastened upon his mind at last, and now, like the absurdity at the heart of all tragedy, a passenger was grabbing him around the waist from behind.

"You've got to save my girlfriend!" he kept screaming. "She's trapped in one of those cabins!" He began trying to push Warms aft toward her cabin. "You've got to save her!"

Fleischman and Hoffman grabbed the hysterical man and tried to explain to him that the captain was trying to save everybody and could not leave the bridge.

"Put him in a boat," Warms said. "Take him down and put him in a boat."

"There's nothing more we can do in the engine room without choking to death," Abbott was saying. "So we're going to shut off everything." He used the plural "we" and yet had not been to the engine room once since the fire started. "Keep the men there by all means," he had told First Engineer Bujia. "Don't let them leave until they have to."

He had heard Warms tell Hackney to lower the boats to the rail, and now, as Warms ran into the wheelhouse to swing the telegraph to Stop All Engines, called after him, "I'm going to leave now."

And he did leave, going right down the bridge ladder on the starboard side to the boat deck, where he got into number three boat. There were only 8 people in it and its capacity was 70 persons, but he shouted, "Lower away!"

"Don't lower that boat!" Warms suddenly began shouting from above. "Keep it at the rail for passengers."

The pelican hook holding it to the deck was jammed and Abbott kept shouting to the seaman, "Kick it! Kick it!"

The seaman finally freed it, but then one of the cables got fouled, making the bow higher than the stern. "This boat is never going down," Abbott said. Then, to Seaman Thomas Charles, as if to spur him on, "We better get away from here or we'll all be burned alive!"

He saw that number one boat, a motor lifeboat with a 58-person capacity, was in operating condition, and so got out of number three and into it.

Dr. Cochrane, the passenger who had lost his sister, was sitting astride the deck rail to protect his bare feet from the hot deck when Abbott passed by him and climbed in. Abbott had been introduced to Dr. Cochrane by Wilmott in the latter's cabin the day before, but it did not occur to Abbott to suggest that Cochrane, a passenger, get into the boat first. He climbed in, sat down on the first thwart at the bow and, wringing his hands and staring at the flames, waited.

Meanwhile Thomas Charles, William Lochmayer and a waiter named Bill Pryor had smashed the window of stateroom 15 on A deck and were attempting to rescue Renee Mendez Capote of Havana, daughter of the first Vice President of Cuba. "The lady's bed was right underneath the window," Charles said, "and all we had to do was to bend in and pick her up. Bill grabbed her feet so she would not be cut with broken glass. We put her in number one with Abbott."

Later, Miss Capote, referring to Pryor, said, "One of the men of the crew was very nice and very brave, and he put me in a lifeboat."

On the bridge, Warms turned to Fleischman: "See what you can do about getting Wilmott's body out. Get it in that boat Abbott's in. Then you take charge."

Fleischman left and Warms hurried to the portside of the bridge. He wanted to see if he'd been right about the breaking of the windows, and he was. Passengers further aft were rushing headlong out of cabins and staterooms as the flames, fed by the gale that the men on the weather side had let in, raced athwart the ship. One passenger cut his chest tumbling out a window he had just broken with his cane. He was without a preserver and as he hopped about, barefoot on the hot deck, his pajamas kept flaking off his back like charred newspaper. The hair had been burned off the back of his head and he kept putting his hand there and looking at the crumbly black evidence and screaming.

Captain Warms ran back to the wheelhouse to ask the engine room why the engines hadn't stopped. But other people around this charred passenger on A deck could not take their eyes off him. The only stability to be found, his wild movements seemed to say, was in momentum, in getting as far as possible away from the fire. He began running toward the stern, grazing the deck rail, bumping into people, tripping over stanchions and ropes.

At the stern rail the compulsion to keep going was so strong that without looking back for another, perhaps less terrifying, glimpse of the fire, he jumped into the propeller-softened water and went down feet first as cleanly as a dish into suds. Finally popping up with the salt burning into his bleeding chest, he went riding down into the deep foaming shallows of the wake, and the people at the stern said later that they could hear him screaming, "I'm here! I'm here! I'm here! I'm here!" as though God were just over the edge of the racing wave and couldn't find him.

Back on the ship, Doris Wacker, the eighteen-year-old girl who had disregarded the steward's advice not to wake her parents ("You'll only cause a panic"), was afraid that she too would soon be forced to jump. "Oh,

Daddy," she said, "what about the lifeboats?"

"If we have to use them," her father said, "someone will surely come and tell us what to do."

Mr. Wacker had been told earlier of considerable drunkenness among members of the ship's personnel. On Wednesday in Havana, the breakfast service had been poor and their dining-room steward had been very much upset about it. When asked what was the matter, the steward had said, "I am willing to do any man's work when he's sick . . . but when they are lying drunk in bunks below, I am not going to help them."

The other side of this story was told by a steward from the *Morro Castle*'s sister ship, the *Oriente:* "Is it surprising that my mates and I drink when we get a chance to? The Ward Line works us eighteen hours a day at sea and we're lucky if we get six hours' leave to see our families when we're in port."

Some men did not care whether they were logged for drunkenness or not. According to the then head of the Seamen's Union, Andrew Furuseth, the profits on smuggled dope from Havana ran so high that these "seamen" actually paid for their jobs instead of receiving wages.

The New York-bound trip was, therefore, the least disciplined trip of the two. Crewmen who knew they were going to quit or be fired often behaved as one waiter did when a passenger, a New York dentist, asked him for lamb chops for his eight-year-old son.

"The waiter said I could not have them," Dr. S. Joseph Bregstein said. "We were very early—about six o'clock. I said, 'Well, there's nothing on the menu he can eat. Will you call the headwaiter?' He said he would, but made no attempt to do so.

"Finally I said, 'Will you call the headwaiter or shall I?' The headwaiter came over and was quite nice about it. He said we would have to wait ten minutes and that he would certainly take care of my request. I had finished my meal and I told my boy to eat his chops when they came. I went out to get some cigarettes from my stateroom. I came back in a few minutes and my boy was just finishing the chops. The waiter asked him how they were. My boy said they were all right, but there was a nail in one of them. He bit into this nail.

"The waiter brought it out to the chef in the kitchen. The chef said he examined the chops before they went out to the dining room and that somebody put the nail in afterwards.

"I was very disappointed with the service. I did not want to complain or criticize as it was just a short trip. But I asked to have my table changed. The headwaiter said he had had trouble with that fellow before; he was not really a waiter—but a dishwasher. The headwaiter said he was going to fire some of the help as he had a good deal of trouble with them."

Adding to the breakdown of manners on the homeward trip was the fraternization in Havana between passengers and crew. The ship was on a Labor Day cruise, when more than the ordinary abundance of widows, schoolteachers, secretaries and college girls ply the Caribbean.

"The American members of the crew made poor sailors on the ship's homeward trip, as they became too familiar with the passengers and couldn't take it when it came to discipline," Isidore Miller, a ballroom steward, said. "If a passenger goes ashore with a bellboy and then later she—well, if that happens, it breaks down the line between passengers and crew. It makes, not for insubordination, exactly, but you can't chase them [the passengers] away."

Second Steward James Pond described the situation this way: "With such a large percentage of women passengers, the possibility exists that a woman would ask a good-looking steward to show her the sights in Havana at her expense."

This line between passengers and crew, as the fire forced more and more people to the stern, broke down completely. Stewards, sailors and officers, many only partly dressed, were indistinguishable from passengers in both appearance and behavior. When a sailor or an officer did show intelligence and leadership, the passengers wouldn't listen.

"I remember one seaman playing a hose on a ladder

to the boat deck and shouting to passengers that if they made a rush for it they could make it to the boats," Steward Daniel Campbell said. "Some tried but hesitated and then ran further aft in fear."

"They refused to go through the smoke and flames," Able-bodied Seaman Leroy Kelsey said. "We pleaded with them, but few of them would go. Many even tried to fight past us and get back down the ladders to the lower decks. The crew urged them to cross the deck and enter the boats, visible through the flames. Sparks and cinders fell about them, and most, becoming confused, refused to risk the few short steps needed to take them to the rail and the safety of the lifeboats."

The older women especially seemed to gravitate to where the only escape from the flames was the ocean itself.

"Shall I jump now?" one such woman asked Doris Wacker.

"I don't know!" Doris Wacker said, and hurriedly turned to her mother, who was murmuring, "Oh, my feet are hot."

Doris put her hand down and felt the deck. It was almost too hot to touch, which seemed to indicate the fire must be beneath them. It wasn't, but since steel is a great conductor of heat, and the deck planking on which she was standing was laid on top of steel, the danger was real of the deck planking bursting into

flame. One factor that made things so difficult at the
stern was that the deck planking on all the weather
decks (Oregon pine, caulked and paved with oakum,
cotton and marine glue) not only had become uncom-
fortable to stand on because of the hot steel beneath it,
but also was giving off suffocating fumes. Finally, when
the marine glue began to ooze out with the heat, people
began to stick and slide in their efforts to free first one
foot, then the other.

"Jump, you women," a few men passengers began
saying. "Why don't you jump? Before it's too late? Get
—overboard!"

They grew bravely insistent, deforming an old tradition of the sea, women and children first, into an ex-
periment. The idea carried forward of the stern, where
the women, if they heeded the advice and jumped,
would be sucked into the propellers and cut to pieces.

"Don't do it!" shouted an officer, forcing his way
forward along the rail, where men, palming off their
fear to utter strangers, were murmuring, "Goodbye. This
is the end. Goodbye."

"I have three children at home," one woman kept
saying. "What are they going to do?"

All the while the officer was grabbing collars and
shoulders in an effort to propel himself forward. "Don't
jump yet. Don't jump! The ship is under way!"

But hysterical women, counting this new urgency as

the product of their own confusion and dread of jumping, got up and jumped from the ship anyway. They tumbled through the air, reaching and clawing with their hands and feet like monkeys bounding from a tree branch by branch. Their bodies smacked against the water and in that instant their cries were snatched from them. People at the rail reached over and strained their eyes and ears, but all was quiet and nothing had happened to the sea.

The officer who had shouted the good advice was now surrounded by a plainting band of women, young and old, in various stages of undress. They were weeping, coughing black mucus into towels and handkerchiefs, and praying. Some—the seasick—vomited.

"Be calm, ladies," the officer said. "Orders will soon be coming from the bridge."

"I—can't swim," one old woman wailed.

"There'll be lifeboats. Now don't worry. You have a preserver."

A man suddenly slipped in among the women to confront the officer. He was fully dressed, in shirt, tie, topcoat and fedora, which gave him the look of an outsider, a marine inspector come to investigate the disaster while it was still in progress.

"Why weren't these people informed of the fire before this?" he demanded. "Why were they brought here and not to the boat deck?"

He overvalued his irritation, displaying all the extravagance of a coward who knows that he is eventually going to break down. Meanwhile it was ridiculous to hold only the captain responsible when this minor officer was here to be attacked directly. In fact, now that he had drawn attention to himself and reminded the women that they, too, deserved better treatment, he found his rage and indignation increasing, and, turning toward the flame-swept bridge, where the captain was presumed to be, raised his fist and shouted, "He should be shot! Shot!"

"One more word," the officer said, "and I'll put you overboard."

"What's that? What's that you said?" But the man's face had changed, so that what he might have said was: Is my pretense up already? Now with his last resource —criticizing others—taken from him, fear raced into his face and filled it. "Look!" he said to the women. "There—look! Do you believe me now?"

It was a lifeboat in the water off the stern, walking stealthily toward shore on six oars. The women watched as it passed through a gleaming play upon the water, and for some reason no one called. There was something inexpressibly repellent in the sight from deck; the boat was less than a fifth occupied. Then it passed into the darkness like the mystery of success in life. What was the secret? How did certain people win?

9

Aboard the *Andrea S. Luckenback,* a freighter in another shipping lane ten miles seaward of the *Morro Castle* and traveling in the same direction, Radio Operator George Silverman was bringing a radio bearing to the captain in the chartroom. Just as he reached the bridge, Second Officer Lang, on the port wing, squinting shoreward through the rain, raised a pair of binoculars to his eyes.

"There seems to be a ship on fire," Lang said.

He handed the binoculars to Silverman, who estimated the distance to be about nine miles. Then the captain stepped out from the chartroom and, taking the binoculars, looked. There was no doubt about it, it was the same large liner they had been paralleling all evening, and the fire appeared to be serious and growing.

The time was 3:10, just twenty minutes after the discovery of the fire on the *Morro Castle,* and already the flames were visible through the rain, nine or ten miles away.

The captain turned to Silverman. "Call the coast station at Tuckerton. Ask them if they know anything about a ship burning off Sea Girt."

Meanwhile, aboard the *Morro Castle,* Rogers was still waiting for Alagna to return from the bridge with orders to send an S O S. The radio room on the *Morro Castle,* located atop the sun (A) deck, was only fifty feet abaft the navigating bridge. Alagna had already shuttled back and forth several times in an attempt to elicit instructions from Warms, but without success. Meanwhile Maki, too, had left the radio room to see how the fire fighters were progressing.

Suddenly, at 3:13 A.M., Alagna slammed in, panting and choking. "The whole place is afire!"

Rogers was one of those men who can both thrive on the tension of others and be made calmer by it. He looked up at Alagna. "What about the distress signal?"

"They're madmen on the bridge and I can't get any co-operation."

But Rogers had turned back to his receiver; something so intensely interesting to him that his whole being seemed to center round it, had come on the air. The *Andrea S. Luckenback,* a freighter, was asking the Tuckerton Station in New Jersey if it had any information about a large liner burning off the coast.

"Do you have any news of a ship burning off Sea Girt?"

Rogers would never forget this conversation. The Tuckerton Station replied, "Haven't heard of any," and that was all; the air was silent again and Rogers sat, cosmic interloper between ignorance and incredulity. The *Luckenback* captain, in another shipping lane but close enough to see the flames, could not understand it; the Tuckerton Station, having received no information, could not enlighten him.

All Rogers would have to have done was cut in on the conversation and say, "Yes, there is a fire—on the *Morro Castle*—and I am awaiting orders from the bridge."

This would not have constituted sending an S O S, which can only be sent on direct orders from the captain, but it would have constituted, technically speaking, an unauthorized message. No admiralty court or grand jury would have failed to understand a human being's desire to tell the *Luckenback* captain that he was not deluded and that it *was* a serious fire he was seeing through ten miles of rain. But Rogers, though poised and deliberate in his actions, was bereft of judgment. The very fact that he chose this moment to obey the law, after breaking it on and off for twenty years, is another indication of the part he may have played in the disaster. For the more he adhered to the rules now, the less likelihood there would be later of his criminal past being brought to light. The investigators would not (and in this case did not) look into the past of the *hero* of the disaster, the one man on the ship who did everything strictly according to the rules governing the behavior of radio operators in a crisis. They would look into the past of a man like Alagna, a ready-made scapegoat who had organized an abortive strike and been accused by the now-dead captain himself (after the captain had spoken to Rogers) of being "vengeful" and determined to "get even."

It was after this *Luckenback* call, *at the urging of Alagna*—who was genuinely concerned about the trapped and screaming passengers and who knew, having already made four trips to the bridge in vain, that an order to send an S O S might never be forthcoming—that Rogers agreed to go on the air with a C Q signal during the silent period, when all ships stand by for emergency calls.

Under international rules the air is silent for three minutes every half hour, starting at the quarter hour and three-quarter hour. During this period ships are required to stand by for emergency messages. The *Luckenback* call to Tuckerton had ended at 3:14 A.M., which meant that the silent period would be starting in less than a minute.

Alagna wet a towel for himself and kept looking at the clock with his flashlight. Only his eyes were visible with the towel over the bridge of his nose and down over his mouth. He looked like some kind of crazy robber, waiting for a safe to blow.

At 3:15 A.M. exactly, his hand tightened round Rogers's shoulder, and the latter came in with a C Q, which is a signal to stand by for an important call. This meant that when and if orders did come from the bridge to send an S O S , they would get aid with the least delay. Rogers started the transmitter and called C Q—C Q —C Q—K G O V, the radio identification of the *Morro Castle*.

Ironically, he was sending the same C Q signal that had led to former Chief Radio Operator Ferson's resignation. Rogers had thought nothing of writing Stanley Ferson those two fraudulent letters urging him, on the basis of an unauthorized C Q signal, to resign, but Rogers himself, in a crisis involving hundreds of lives, had to be urged by Alagna to send the same unauthorized C Q signal. The difference was that the fraud had been anonymous and this unauthorized C Q signal wasn't.

The Tuckerton Station, alerted by the *Luckenback* call for information, broke in immediately with, "K G O V, wait three minutes."

Of course Rogers knew what they were thinking: that the *Morro Castle* had seen the flaming ship, too. They were warning him to stay out of the silent period so that the flaming ship could use it. So he wired back: "No, O R X-K G O V," meaning the emergency was on the *Morro Castle*.

The Tuckerton Station shut up then, and for three of the longest minutes in maritime history, they waited for orders from the bridge to send an S O S. Just before the silent period was due to end, Alagna suggested sending the signal and information again, and just as Rogers finished sending it, the main transmitter, run by engine-room power, ceased functioning. The whole ship was in darkness now and they could hear the cries of dismay rise from all over.

"George, unscrew the emergency lamp and see if it's burned out," Rogers said. He never lost his temper and never shouted, this huge burly man with the well-insulated nervous system. His mind was so clear, and so disassociated from his emotions, that he was able to give every mechanical detail his undivided attention. He might have been in a laboratory far beneath the surface of the earth.

He got a flashlight from a drawer and went to the auxiliary transmitter, which was controlled independently of everything else by the two batteries in the radio room. He began setting it up with Alagna, who reached over and threw in the auxiliary transmitter switch on the panel board and transferred the antenna from the main switch to the auxiliary. Both of them, while they worked, kept trying instinctively to find clean, unblackened places in their towels to breathe through.

Meanwhile, the gasoline on deck, overheated by the fire that its own vapors had spread, was squirting all over the deck and being washed by the rain down into the cabins below and onto the thick drapes and rugs and highly varnished fittings that a comfort-loving public demands of every shipping company.

"All right, get to the bridge," Rogers said as soon as they had the auxiliary transmitter set up. "And come back with orders."

"Give me my hat," Alagna said. "I don't think Warms knows who I am!"

The people were gone from this part of the ship now; all Rogers could hear as Alagna slammed out was the silken whirr of the flames. He became conscious that his feet were blistering and when he put his hand to the fireproof Selbalith flooring he found it too hot to touch.

He put his feet up on the rung of his chair and then noticed, when he put his searchlight on it, that the bulkhead separating the radio and emergency rooms showed discoloration (the gas from the tanks had caught fire). Then a shift in the wind blew the fire through the porthole, and the settee under it started burning.

He tried to put it out, but it was no use; and besides, the deck burned his feet when he stood up. So he went back to the emergency transmitter, put the earphones on, and sat with his feet up on the rung waiting for Alagna.

Perhaps the strongest argument against fires at sea being started deliberately is that the firesetter has no more assurance that he will escape with his life than anyone else on the ship. This argument is a sound one except in the case of a pathological firesetter, who, while under the influence of his irresistible impulse, does not care whether he lives or dies. Once the fire is set, he often becomes passive, as though his tension, too, were expiring in the flames.

As Rogers waited, the flames spread round the steel housing in which he sat. The earphones clamped round his ears were absolutely silent except for the static from the heat of the ship setting up disturbances.

10

When Stop All Engines rang in the engine room, oilers and firemen had already abandoned their posts. Though they had prepared the machinery for the shut down that they knew was imminent, they had at the last moment left the final task to Third Engineer Arthur Stamper, whose misfortune it was to be in charge of the engine room at the time.

In the darkness and smoke it was as if the ship designer's hand itself had Stamper by the throat. For what had driven the others out was not fire (the fire was in the superstructure) but smoke, which had been sucked in through a ventilating system designed to run as long as the electric motors turned the propellers. This ventilation, used as a forced draft to keep the electric driving apparatus cool, was geared so that it could be shut off only by stopping the ship.

He groped among the clocks and dials and countless gauges, pushing wrong buttons and pulling wrong switches until the machinery, pounding out its 1600-shaft horsepower, began to shake the deck beneath him. Stopping the main propulsion motors came first because he could no longer communicate with the bridge and he wanted to save as much steam as possible for the fire-line pump.

Even with his flashlight he could barely see through the smoke, and what increased his rage and desperation was that the noise of the very motors he was trying to stop tore at his study of the vast control board. A certain delicacy was required to shut down a million dollars' worth of machinery. Wheels had to be turned, switches pulled; other more sensitive instruments would break if the pressure brought to bear on them were angry pressure. With bated breath he cursed this crying need for industry in the black belly of a ship.

"Stamper!" It was First Engineer Anthony Bujia, calling down to him from the grating level on E deck. "Secure the boilers and shut down. Leave the feed pump and fire pump running and get out."

Stamper, on the operating platform between the telephone booth and a ladder leading down to the lower engine room, pointed his flashlight at Bujia. There was a moment's hesitation, then Stamper started down the ladder to the lower engine room, the flashlight illuminating his rung-by-rung descent, whereupon Bujia, following Abbott's example, also left. The traditions of the sea were intentionally made a little too severe, it would seem, in the hope that in a crisis someone like this suffocating Stamper might take them seriously and thereby break the chain reaction toward panic.

Stamper got down on his hands and knees and began breathing the less-contaminated air off the corrugated floors, crawling and looking, crawling and looking, like some Gargantuan metal-eating termite. There they were, like glowing rulers, the under-rims of the boiler doors. He crawled over to them and reared into the denser smoke, closing his eyes against it and feeling with his hands. Just then someone came reeling through the smoke and bumped into him. It was Junior Engineer Lewis Wright, still on duty in the fireroom.

"Shut—the—fires—off!" Stamper choked through the blackness. "And cut off the oil to the boilers. Here"—he gave Wright the flashlight—"I'll be right back."

Stamper had already stopped the main propulsion motors but not the turbines, and that's what he wanted

to go back to the main engine room for. The smoke outside the fireroom had grown so much worse that, like a
blind man, he retained his sense of direction only by the
feel of things and by approximating the number of steps
from one thing to another. Finally, when he dropped
the bars that tripped the turbines, one on one side and
one on the other, the absolute silence that followed
seemed to hesitate before entering where so much noise
had been.

For some reason he became more aware of the ship's
movement as the silence took on personality, and less
able to get the feel of that movement in his legs. It was
another thing to think of, a presage of what was going
on above. (Had they let go the anchor? Was she swinging head on to the storm?) But there were already too
many things to think about, and he was choking, taking headers through the darkness and finding things,
the wrong things, to hit every time. He knew that if
Wright didn't turn the boilers off, the ship would blow
up; and this terrible knowledge in the darkness, the roll
and movement of the ship, the banging of waves against
her hull and the bayou wash of water in the bilges, became a kind of dirge, accompanying the dead earnestness of his intentions. It was as if the ship were express-
ing in some leviathan language of distress her great
need of him. There was a somber, longing eloquence in

her sounds that made him resist the fear that all men have of dying in the hole, where the iron sky you throw your last words to throws them back.

Reeling back into the fireroom, he hollered, "You shut off the oil-stop valves? . . . You sure? . . . Every one?" And when Wright said "yes" each time: "Here, come here. Shut the steam off this fuel-oil pump. I'll hold the flashlight for you."

The point was to turn the fuel off and then set the steam valves so that the fire pump would run as long as any pressure remained in the huge boilers. The second task, the steam valves, Stamper might have ignored, for he was choking to death and the primary task, turning the fuel off to prevent an explosion, was done. But he knew that there would be no water to fight the fire if he didn't set the steam valves right, so he held the flashlight up next to the fire-pump pressure gauge. The arrow was swinging between 85 and 90 pounds and he opened the throttle to boost it up a little more. Then he went to the main steam pump and opened the steam pressure up on that a little, too.

He had been panting with exertion, pulling the resinous poison into his mouth because his nostrils had clogged, and now, with nothing left to do but escape, he reverted to exhaustion and defeat and felt an almost drunken temptation to lie down.

Wright grabbed him by the arm. "Is that all? Come on!"

Recruiting the very last of his energies, Stamper staggered out of the fireroom with Wright and called, "Anybody here?" whereupon smaller and smaller voices echoed the same thing: "Anybody here?" "Anybody here?" "Anybody here?"

Stamper knew there was no escape upward, because earlier, when he'd told Cadet Engineer Tripp to go up and wake the engineers, Tripp had come back and said, "I can't get out the door on top; it's on fire up there."

"The tunnel," Stamper said, clutching at Wright's arm. "Come on!"

They crawled over, closing and opening their eyes against smoke. At the tunnel that housed the shafts leading aft to the propellers, they helped each other in with a pawing brutal fondness, each staying alive by keeping the other alive.

The tunnel, too, was filled with smoke, but the farther they crawled through it, the clearer the air got and the stronger they grew. Their oxygen-happy hearts sweetened their blood again, sweetened life. Stamper was even positive he could hear singing, but he didn't say anything for fear Wright would think he was crazy. It was a maturation process, this crawl to fresher air; they filled their lungs, grew taller and broader as they walked, were men again as they climbed to D deck on the bouncing stern and found twenty-odd passengers hysterically singing, "Hail, Hail, the Gang's All Here," in a last ditch effort to hold on to their wits. There were men in underwear among them, girls in high heels and long trailing evening gowns, and women on their knees, who were literally tearing their hair out as they sang. Trying to calm them was a tan girl in a red Jantzen bathing suit (someone later recalled the tiny sun-lit diving girl trademark), and for a moment Stamper thought the ship had backed onto one of the beaches along the Jersey shore and the girl, an eager-beaver sight-seer or something, had swum out to see if she could help.

But he was wrong, for no sooner did the passengers see him—charcoal gray except for his white-rimmed eyes—than they associated him with the engine room and, like savages, left off singing to spear him with their fears.

"Will the ship blow up?" "Should we jump now?" "Where are the lifeboats?" "Is help coming?" "Help us! Help us! Please!" All shouted at once, with a wailing primitiveness that made him, in spite of everything, feel lucky. These people had not been denied the last extremity of fear, as he had been with duties to perform and the gumption to perform them. It was a lesson to be learned even now; he looked behind him, the fire was perhaps fifty feet away and burning toward them.

They would all have to jump soon if it couldn't be contained.

"The ship will not blow up," he said. "I can promise you that. Now be calm, and don't jump until you have to. Maybe you won't have to."

He got the men passengers to help him swing out a hose, went with the nozzle as close as he could get to the fire and told one of the men to turn the valve. They were down low, on D deck, and the water pressure was still pretty good. He soaked the walls and fixtures that had not yet caught fire and directed streams at the ceiling to prevent the flames from working downward. His work with the steam valves in the engine room earlier was now saving his life and the lives of others.

"Turn it off!" Stamper shouted every now and again. "Don't waste it."

During lulls he would look around at the crazy variety show of life preservers over evening gowns and coats and try to persuade the women to be sensible. "Your clothes'll pull you under if you jump. Take 'em off! Your preservers won't do any good with that weight." He pointed to the girl in the bathing suit. "Look!"

Then he would ask for more water, while first one, and then another woman would remove her dress and slippers and put her preserver back on over her slip. Many, in the midst of panic, carefully arranged their clothing—with their compacts, cigarettes and matches tucked in their shoes—in the hope they would not have to abandon ship. The more carefully they arranged their clothes, it seemed, the more their hope revived.

The Morro Castle *before the fire at sea.*

The great pleasure ship on fire.

Passengers hang from ropes as they wait for rescuers.

TOP: *Survivors, as they approach the* Monarch of Bermuda.

BOTTOM: *Residents of Spring Lake, N. J., greet the first lifeboat to reach shore.*

TOP: *The boat deck—with an unlaunched lifeboat.*

BOTTOM: *One of the enclosed decks after the fire.*

A lifeboat that never got lowered

RIGHT TOP: *The scarred liner beached at Asbury Park.*   Wide World

RIGHT MIDDLE: *Salvagers tried to free the charred hulk. The* Morro Castle
three months after the disaster.   UPI

RIGHT BOTTOM: *A close-up of the beached vessel, with crowds of sight-seers*

What remained of the Castle's *superstructure—complete with unlaunched
lifeboat.*

Chief Radio Operator George W. Rogers gives his testimony during the Federal inquiry in New York.

Rogers in 1938 . . . and 1953, after the Hummel murders.

11

"Warms, you coming?" Abbott kept shouting to the bridge from number one boat. When he received no answer, he turned to the seamen. "Lower away! For God's sake, lower away!"

Waiting in the boat for over ten minutes, and knowing that he could not remain in it and lower it into the water, too, he'd become half crazed with fear and frustration. The Melin-Macklachlan gravity davits were designed to prevent the premature lowering of a boat by the panic-stricken: they could be operated only from the deck of the ship. Abbott knew all about the idea behind that design and the knowledge only added to his panic. "Lower away!" he kept shouting. "Will someone, for God's sake, lower away?"

Warms, on the bridge, was distracted from Abbott's wailing by a tremendous blast on the portside of the ship. It was the ship's Lyle gun, falling through the gutted deck into the heart of the fire below. In the confusion no one had remembered to throw the pretzel can of gunpowder overboard.

"It fell through the deck into the middle of the fire," Howard Hansen said, "and twenty pounds of powder went off, blowing everything apart, all the windows and some doors and walls, and putting an end to the firefighting. I saw three of the crew killed and four passengers jump over the side, so I decided it was about time to abandon ship."

Warms heard the growing tumult and screams for help, and experienced an anguish such as he had never known. He was not only losing his ship, not only unable to get his passengers off safely, but they, in turn, were beginning to fight one another. Nothing seemed left of the world's goodness but the bouyancy of this horror ship, and only an hour before he'd felt his pleasure running like the very water fore and aft.

He had reached the point where he was no longer concentrating on how to extinguish the fire but on the fire itself. There were so many flames, all of them so

hopelessly out of control, that no one flame demanded
his special attention. His fear of the ship's destruction
had grown to sheer, naked anxiety, so that just getting
back to fear would have been an accomplishment—a
spur to action. But there was nothing to be done; the
maniacal flames had captured the ship.

A man was shouting in his ear, "Captain, listen to me.
What about a distress signal?" It was Alagna, standing
in the glow of the fire so Warms could see his radio
officer's hat. He had been shouting against the wind and
crackling flames until his teeth had almost bitten into
the lobe of Warms's ear. "Rogers is *dying* in there! He
can't hold out much longer. What do you want us to
do?"

Warms turned and looked at him, but it was as if
nothing could be of consequence any more.

"A ship has sighted us from a long distance!" Alagna
went on.

The first mate aboard the *Luckenback,* Frank Magruder, said afterward that when he first looked through
glasses at the burning ship (shortly after three), "the
vessel, aflame from the fore part of her superstructure
all the way aft to the break of the superstructure, was
still traveling in a northerly direction." This contra-
dicted Warms's claim that he turned the ship away
from the wind immediately on being told that there
was a fire in the writing room. If Magruder's eyes were

not deceiving him, the *Morro Castle* traveled into a head wind for almost fifteen minutes after the fire was discovered.

"A ship has sighted us!" Alagna repeated.

It was at this point, he said later, that an inspiration seemed to cross Warms's face. There was one last hope to hurl at despair. "Is there still time to send an S O S?"

"Yes!"

"Send it!"

Alagna grabbed him, determined not to lose his attention now that he'd attracted it. "What position?"

"Twenty miles south of Scotland Light. About eight miles off coast."

Quartermaster Fleischman, returning to tell Warms that he could not get Wilmott's body out because of the flames, heard the order and repeated it: "Twenty miles south of Scotland Light. About eight miles off coast." Then Quartermaster Hoffman repeated it, and Warms, as if reverting by rote to ship's routine, called out, "What time is it?"

Fleischman sang out, "Three eighteen," and Hoffman repeated it, so the S O S order was given at precisely 3:18, or approximately fifteen minutes after the fire had been reported out of control. This fifteen minute delay in sending out an S O S, much discussed by mariners afterwards, constituted Warms's third major mistake. He had failed to instruct his men to close the fire-screen doors, failed to turn the ship away from the wind in an effort to confine the fire at its point of origin, and waited fifteen unnecessary minutes to send an S O S. All were errors in judgment made by a man under extraordinary emotional stress, a man who had to think of a hundred things at once and who would have been scorned (afterwards) if he'd asked for advice. There was no purser to help him, no chief steward, and no "four-striper" like Eban S. Abbott.

It is ironic that the invention of the wireless, which in this case was to mean the saving of hundreds of lives, has actually helped to prevent captains of ships from reaching their true and full development as men. In a time of crisis like this one, a captain is alone; there is no one he can turn to but himself. During ordinary runs since the invention of the wireless, however, he is expected by his company to call the home office for orders in much the same way that a salesman or company representative might. He is expected to have small initiative in commercial matters, and then be a god of calmness and control at a time like this.

Alagna started toward the radio room, but in his effort to avoid the flames he lost his sense of direction. Not until his back touched the bridge rail and he climbed down and stumbled into the chartroom did he know where he was.

"I'm a radio officer," he said to Fleischman, who suddenly bumped into him in the darkness and smoke. "Radio officer!" No one on the bridge seemed to know who he was. "I can't get to the radio room."

Fleischman led him by flashlight to the telephone in the wheelhouse, pressed the button for the radio room, handed him the receiver and left with the flashlight. But Alagna could not hear the buzzing that would indicate the bell on the other end was ringing, and suddenly he realized that all the ship's electrical power had burned out. He reeled back into the smoke, dazed and choking. God help Rogers, he thought, looking aft through the flames. God help him.

Meanwhile, everybody in the vicinity of number one boat—Renee Capote of Havana, Paul Arneth of Brooklyn, Dr. Cochrane and several burned and choking seamen—had already climbed in or been put in, the heat having made it impossible to remain on deck.

"That's all, Hoffman," Warms was saying to his loyal quartermaster on the bridge. He gave him a tap on the shoulder. "Hurry before it's too late."

"I'll stick with you," Hoffman said.

"You better get out of here, son, while you can." He turned, told Fleischman the same thing and added, "Get in number one boat and take charge."

The two quartermasters started to leave, but at the

rail, before they descended to the boat deck, Fleischman said to Hoffman, "God damn it, if he can stay, we can stay."

A sudden burst of flame changed their minds for them, and Hoffman said later, "I ran to the port wing and saw a mass of flames like a furnace out there. I went back to the starboard side, and at that time there was a big cloud of smoke. Flames came like torches out of the doors there. The radio shack and bridge deck were aflame and from there I sort of vaulted off the bridge onto A deck and was helped into number three boat by Able-bodied Seaman Bill Bernhardt. The boat stopped at B deck on the way down; glass was popping and it was a furnace. A human being couldn't live in that. We hit the water and they were all screeching and howling."

When Clarence Hackney finally began lowering number one boat (Fleischman, too, had climbed in), it was so hot from the flames that when the people in it coughed and spit, their saliva sizzled against the metal. Then the rear davit jammed, throwing the boat at such an angle that everybody burned his hands trying not to tumble into the water.

"Wait, I'll get it." A young seaman wearing blue dungarees jumped out of the boat to help lower it down. He stayed with the davit until the boat was waterborne and the falls went slack, then scrambled over to the Jacob's ladder to climb down into the boat before it got clear of the side of the ship. He was only halfway down the Jacob's ladder, however, when the unhooked boat was taken by a wave and carried about ten feet from the side of the ship.

The young seaman didn't hesitate—broken glass and huge flaps of hot paint were showering down on him from above—he jumped and immediately began swimming toward the boat while those in it shouted encouragement and held out oars for him.

A half-empty boat has such an unpredictable way of behaving in a roughly racing sea, however, that for someone trying to reach it in the water its very haphazard bouyancy can become an object first of fury, then of heart-consuming hate. There were times when he was literally swimming uphill toward it, when it was ten feet higher than he was; and other times when, it seemed, if he could have jumped out of the water, he would have fallen right into the boat. His shipmates strained with their outstretched oars to reach him, and though his hand once came to within a foot of one of the blades, he started to lose ground the harder he tried to regain it.

And all during these efforts to save the man without whose help the boat might never have reached the water, Abbott was sitting not two feet away from a coil of rope. "He was probably sitting on it," Fleischman said later.

The rope, a painter, was over a hundred feet long. Someone might have cast it from the boat, or jumped from the boat with one end (the other end made fast) and saved the young man's life.

"Try to start that motor!" Fleischman shouted round.

Abbott was sitting just forward of the motor, but did nothing until Percy Miller, an electrician, took the cover off and began working on it. After he'd cranked it a few times, there was a smell of gas, and Abbott said (in an "unusual" voice, according to Fred Walther, the ordinary seaman sitting next to him), "Don't start it. There are too many sparks coming from the ship. Don't start it."

Had the motor been fixed, the boat might have circled the ship and picked up passengers struggling in the water. But Chief Engineer Abbott lay across the thwarts at the bow, temporarily a dead man.

"Why don't you take an oar and row?" Fred Walther asked him.

"I can't. I cut my hand."

Then Abbott did a very strange thing, indeed. He turned his palm to Walther. Only there was no cut.

Did he turn up the wrong hand? Or was his anxiety so great that he both believed he had a cut of a special unknown type and that Walther could see it? It was al-

most as if anxiety had stimulated some creative poten-
tiality in the man. He was using his imagination as he
had probably never used it before, and would probably
never use it again. The very conflict with reality made
him innocent.

12

Alagna, meanwhile, having abandoned the telephone as a means of getting the S O S order to Rogers, was still trying to reach him. He tried the portside, then the starboard, but now between him and the radio room was such a sea of flame that the ship might have been made of wood and not steel at all.

It was now 3:20, only thirty minutes after the discovery of the fire in the writing room, and the entire superstructure was ablaze. The charges of negligence and cowardice against members of the crew are explained by this unheard-of speed of the fire's spread.

Passengers who had been roused from sleep at three, or five minutes after, could not believe that the fire had not been raging for hours. Why had the crew waited so long, they wanted to know, before coming to their aid? But the crewmen, roused to subdue a fire already out of control, said that they were themselves taken by surprise. The only explanation is that the fire was carefully and deliberately set.

Alagna stumbled down a companionway to A deck. Choking and half blind from the smoke, he began wondering whether Rogers would be alive even if he could still get to him. He doubted it, but then when the ship, swinging on its anchor, caught a freak twist of wind, a passage was blown through the flames and he immediately thought that Rogers might be alive after all. He ran aft through the clearing, but it was no use. The smoke was like another kind of darkness; it allowed no light, no air, no life at all. He began to smother and to regret having come back, when suddenly, confronted by the flames again, he realized he had gone past the radio room.

Turning back he saw, or thought he saw, through a sudden lurch of smoke, Rogers's flashlight. It was like a reminder that he, too, was still conscious and he ran toward it shouting, "Send the S O S! We're twenty miles south of Scotland Light."

Rogers's fingers were already on the keys: S O S—
S O S—K G O V. Twenty miles south of Scotland Light.

He was only halfway through the message when a
corner of the radio room exploded. There was a loud
puff and a flash of light; the room filled with sulphuric
gas from the battery solution. Boiling acid spilled over
the floor and around the chair on whose rung Rogers
had his feet. The receivers were out of commission, but
Rogers continued to send the S O S because the transmitter was still running.

He didn't realize it, but his position—twenty miles
south of Scotland Light—had been missed by those
listening in because of the static sent up by the heat of
the ship. Harrison W. Batchelder at the Tuckerton Station in New Jersey, though he had received the S O S,
did not know as yet where to send help.

Sydney E. Jones, the Radio Operator on the *Monarch
of Bermuda,* a British ship about thirty miles from the
Morro Castle, found himself in the same predicament.
He too had received the S O S, but it was broken up or
interfered with by other ships. "There was the S O S,"
Jones said, "then some words lost due to interference.
Then came the words, 'About twenty miles south of
——' and then a word, 'otland' . . . an abbreviation for
light vessel. But the message was broken up and useless
as it stood."

If at this point, therefore, Rogers and Alagna had abandoned the radio room, at least three hundred more people would have died than did die. The extremity of the moment actually added to Rogers's self-control; he got up and staggered through the acid bubbling on the hot floor to the switchboard. The small auxiliary generator had stopped and he wanted to see if a wire had come loose. There was no way of seeing, so he felt with his hands, thinking the heat might have melted the solder around a connection. He found one loose, all right, and began shaping it around a lug—so thoroughly, so carefully—that it was good it was dark and Alagna couldn't see him. Alagna might otherwise have cut his own throat rather than go on watching him.

The generator started again and Rogers, staggering around, only later remembered that when he finally found the table again and sat down, his feet burned even when he put them up on the rung. The acid had soaked into his shoes and was eating into the blisters on his feet. He was losing consciousness gradually and when he fell over the table, it was only the radio key, digging into his forehead, that brought him to. He put his fingers to it and at exactly 3:26, on the *Monarch of Bermuda,* this is the message Sydney E. Jones received:

C Q—S O S—Twenty miles south of Scotland Light. Cannot work much longer. Fire directly under radio. Need assistance immediately.

Then there was an explosion in the *Morro Castle*'s generator set and the sender stopped for good.

Rogers lay across the table, thinking, he recalled later: If I'm supposed to be dying, it doesn't hurt much. I'm just getting sleepy.

Alagna grabbed him by the shoulders. "The whole place is afire. Come on!"

The S O S had been sent; both the sender and the receiver were dead; there was no earthly reason for them to remain. But Rogers was still apparently thinking of the rules governing the behavior of radio operators in a crisis.

"Go back to the bridge," he said, "and see if there's anything else?"

What else could there be but the parade in his honor through the streets of Bayonne? He leaned over the keyboard again and, "waiting for Alagna to come back with orders, passed into unconsciousness."

Alagna realized it would be impossible to live here another two minutes; going back to the bridge would mean both their lives. He grabbed Rogers and shook him. "Warms says we are to abandon ship. Let's go!"

Rogers allowed his huge 250-pound frame to be propelled through the door. On deck he got hold of the starboard rail and pulled himself up. The fire was hard not to look at; it was everywhere, unbelievably complete and furious—a sea of flame. But he got to the pilothouse (the ship appeared to be anchored), and found it empty and already beginning to burn. He went over to the gyrocompass and, looking down the officers' hallway, saw that he was standing above a raging fire. He could barely bring himself to leave. His mind was clear, and he afterward remembered this moment of standing above the flames that were consuming Captain Wilmott's body.

He managed to get back to the starboard wing of the bridge, where there was a companionway leading down, and was detained by the outline of empty davits running aft along the boat deck. They hung empty over the water, aglow with heat.

"And all the while, just below and a little aft of where I was standing," he said later, "three men had hold of something dark and were trying to throw it overboard. The flames were all around them, but they were very intent."

"This way, chief," Alagna was saying, "this way."

They got to A deck where the heat coming off the steel was enough to burn one's cheeks. There were crashing "bams" as portholes blew; the crackling and snapping of wood; sudden "pows" of paint blisters breaking, and from inside the superstructure, muffled blasts of demijohns of rum exploding. Deck plates buckled and pulled red-hot rivets up with them; elevator shafts and mail chutes twisted out of line; the steel frames of beds warped out sounds; hose nozzles, their canvas hoses long since gone up in smoke, rolled like hot skewers over the deck. It was the inanimate world speaking, and its sheer inexorable timing was almost more than one could bear. The glass in a porthole blew as the heat became too much for it; doorknobs oxidized; cans of polish exploded; paint peeled off metal and the metal itself turned red.

Alagna called again and finally Rogers saw him. They couldn't find the ladder leading to the foredeck and so shook hands and said they might meet again.

"Well," Rogers said, "it looks like we're the only two who kept our heads. There is nothing for us to be ashamed of. We waited for orders to send an S O S and sent it."

The deck below, which led to the bow, was a twenty-foot drop and it was only a matter of seconds how long they could stand where they were. Alagna said he was going to jump, even if it meant breaking his leg, but Rogers said he was going to hang by his hands to shorten the drop, even if it meant burning his hands. They had a kind of disagreement, all the more weird for being reasonable with the fire about to loot them of their clothes. Then the ship rolled and they looked under the floor of smoke and saw the ladder rungs. They got to them, climbed down, and started for the forepeak.

Captain Warms was there with about a dozen others,

officers and crew, and Dr. Vosseler and his wife, who had been told by Ordinary Seaman Charles Angelo, when the fire first started, to "go forward. It's safe up there."

Warms couldn't take his eyes off the flaming superstructure. "Is it real or am I dreaming?" he kept saying. "Is it real or am I dreaming?"

The ship was now divided in two, with the captain and officers at the bow, the passengers at the stern. The superstructure was like an apartment house on fire and there were arms waving out ports to which no one could go and from which no one could escape. The arms waved less frantically after a while, then disappeared as the flames erupted.

The officers could not help it, but the same wind that was protecting them from the fire was bringing it closer and closer to the passengers.

13

At the stern women cried frantically for children who were sometimes no more than two feet away; men fought for preservers for their wives, sailors with nothing else to do cursed. And all during the confusion, authoritative voices could be heard saying things like, "Keep off all metal objects. They will be charged."

One barefoot man in a Basque shirt and white duck trousers had had his hand cut off by a snapped cable and was using the other as a tourniquet. He padded about with appalling calmness, both arms straight out as though he were asking for alms with the missing hand. "Who has a gun?" he said as two men began ripping their shirts in an effort to help him. "I heard a shot."

Lewis Perrone, making his way toward the stern along the portside of the ship, heard it, too. Still wearing the white mess jacket he had put on for the party in cabin 237, he was bending low under a port for fear it might splinter in his face, when he heard what sounded like the crack of a pistol. Turning, he saw an officer and a sailor. They must have stepped out on deck from inside the superstructure, because Perrone had just sidled past that part of the ship. The officer had a gun in his hand and the sailor was lying in a prone position on the deck before him. Perrone did not actually see the officer shoot the sailor—indeed saw nothing until after he had heard the shot—but the next day a seaman was washed ashore with a bullet in his eye and two hundred dollars in his pocket—a looter, the papers said.

At the rail on C deck, some young people were just beginning to sing in an effort to bolster one another, when a man called over, "Don't sing. Say your prayers."

Adele Brady was there and heard him. She was with her husband and seventeen-year-old daughter, Nancy, who finally reached a man in a white uniform, the assistant purser, and said, "Is it time to jump?"

"I guess you could."

"How should I jump?"

"I would jump facing the boat."

Edward Brady helped his wife to the top of the rail, where she hesitated and said, "If I go, will you come?"

Mr. Brady, who had been ill and for whose sake they had taken the Havana cruise, choked up and couldn't speak. Save yourself, his expression seemed to say, don't think of me. But his wife insisted, "Will you?" and Ed Brady, nodding, waited until she jumped, then jumped in after her.

They were mostly alone in the water ("It was fearfully cold," Mrs. Brady said later), but dead bodies floated by and occasionally they saw live people they had known as passengers. Mrs. Brady wasn't certain who they were because everybody looked so different in the water. The man who had eaten his meals at the table next to theirs, now gasping for breath every time a wave passed over him, just didn't look like the same man. When Mr. Lyon came by, semiconscious and with his head hanging over the edge of his preserver, they reached out to see if they could help. Something appeared to be wrong with his neck; he couldn't hold his head up to get air. There was nothing they could do, but Adele Brady held his hand until he died.

Back on deck, the man was still insisting that everybody pray. "You should not sing at a time like this," he said, "you should pray."

"So we all prayed," said Martha Bradbury, a hospital

nurse at Columbia Presbyterian Medical Center in New York City. "I know I never prayed so hard in my life. Finally we got to the rail and the flames were so close there was nothing to do but jump. The water was very cold. We tried to move our arms and legs as rapidly as possible to keep warm. We swam and swam. We could see the lights of ships and in the distance we could see shore. We swam and swam and swam, but we didn't seem any closer to anything.

"Then my friend Lillian Davidson said to me, 'Martha, I can't hold out much longer.'

"I shouted to her to encourage her. But a few minutes later I looked for her and she had disappeared. I kept on swimming and swimming and praying and praying and several times I almost gave up. Then I thought: Oh, what the hell's the use of giving up? So I kept on swimming, and one time a dead body floated right by me. But I thought: Where there's life there's hope. So I kept on swimming."

On the ship, another passenger, David Schneider, who had carried a little Cuban girl in a plaid silk dress to safety outside the superstructure (he was in textiles himself and vividly remembered the dress as being plaid silk), was saying to the assistant purser, "There are a lot of old women and children around here without preservers. Will you give me yours?" He pointed to a particularly old woman leaning against the rail.

"I'm sorry, I can't swim," the assistant purser said. "I need the preserver myself."

He waited until Mr. Schneider turned, then slipped away, brushing past Dr. Gouverneur Morris Phelps, who was staring intently toward the New Jersey shore off which he had cruised and fished for years.

"Katherine," he said to his wife, "that light over yonder must be Scotland Light and that one over there must be Ambrose. That means the beach over there must be less than seven miles away. I know this part of the coast. The wind is blowing directly toward shore. I think, dear, our only chance is to go over and try to make the beach on our own. Will you come?"

Mrs. Phelps smiled through her tears and nodded. She was standing next to a Cuban passenger, Rafael Mestre, who had overheard the doctor and was secretly making a bargain with himself to jump if Mrs. Phelps did.

"Gouvie," the doctor said to his son. "I have all I can do to take care of your mother. You're a man now. You can take care of yourself."

A few minutes before, young Phelps had given his father his preserver, saying he had another, and Dr. Phelps had believed him. ("I would never have taken it if I'd known . . .")

"Don't wait too long," the doctor went on. "Promise me you'll go over before that partition burns through. Good luck, boy."

Young Phelps said later, "The wind was high. He talked into my ear. There was no shaking of hands. The fire threatened to break through the second-class dining-salon partition at any moment." Dr. Phelps lifted his wife over the rail and let her drop into the water. The stern lifted under the heave of a strong wave and then he went over after her. "I thought I heard the splash when he hit. He's six feet, and weighs two hundred."

About thirty yards away from the ship, Dr. Phelps found a mattress and pulled himself up on it "the better to look for my wife." While he was looking, he heard a little voice that he recognized and she swam to him. She had hold of a piece of charred wood and was using it as one might a float, kicking with her feet and holding on with her hands.

Meanwhile other people who had jumped were making for the sopping raft. "You'll only sink it," warned Dr. Phelps from his puddled cavity in the middle. They ignored him and held on until the doctor was eased down into the black water with them.

On the ship, the flames were beginning to break through the dining-salon partition. They tongued up as from an open well and got into the hangings in the lounge and into the piles of costumes and uniforms. A dense smoke followed as the costumes caught, so black and blinding that Robert Smith, the cruise director, immediately began shouting, "You have preservers. Jump! Let your children go over first. Please hurry!"

Only those at the rail were able to breathe. The others, choking and half blind from the smoke, wanted only to get to the rail and jump before they were overcome. Rosario Comacho and Francesco [Franz] Hoed, an eighteen-year-old Cuban on his way north to enter Columbia University, had almost reached the rail when they realized that the man directly in front of them had no intention of jumping.

"Because of his height," Miss Comacho said, "he could lean over the rail and breathe comfortably without abandoning the ship. Our frantic coughing and desperate pulls at his shirt did not and could not dislodge him. Finally, as everything turned black before my eyes and I began losing consciousness, I did what later astounded me.

"With Franz pushing me and total suffocation only seconds away, I thrust my face forward with my mouth wide open and, before I knew what had happened, there were my good strong teeth burying themselves in the fleshiest part of that man's upper back! He turned and reeled backwards, with a loud scream of pain, and it was this flash-like clearance that offered us the opportunity to climb the rail, take one deep breath of fresh air, and, holding hands, brace ourselves for the thirty-foot jump.

"Just as we were about to leap, a gasping old man lost his balance on top of the rail and, colliding with Franz, knocked us apart. As I went down screaming Franz's name, I distinctly remember him flying through the air looking for me. And that was the last I saw of him, or of anyone else, because oblivion overtook me even before I hit the water.

"I have no way of knowing how long I remained unconscious, although I do remember that my first awareness was of a penetratingly cold surrounding liquid, furiously pushing and pulling me back and forth. . . . I also remember someone addressing himself to me, and believing it was Franz I redoubled my efforts to wake up. Someone who seemed totally alien to me, but with my voice, asked the person who had addressed himself to me for his name. 'I don't know you!' this same girl with my voice kept saying, 'Where am I? Don't speak to me because I don't know you.'

"Something serious had happened to me, to my mind. Who was I? Was I returning from France? Or was I going there? What was my name and where did I fit? Had I a family? I must [have].

"All these questions, and hundreds more, raced through my brain until, suddenly, I opened my eyes— they had been so heavy!—and, looking up toward the blazing ship, saw the words *'Morro Castle'* above me. But of my own identity I still knew nothing. Then, continuing my efforts to remember, I saw first my father standing at the pier waving, then my mother, which was exactly how I had last seen them. I clearly recalled their names, and then without any further effort, my own. This gave me a new hold on myself, making me feel fortified and as if protected."

Back on the ship Cruise Director Robert Smith, with ever-increasing urgency, was telling all passengers with preservers to jump. Mrs. Ruben Holden of Cincinnati kissed her husband and bent down to kiss her sons, John, twelve, and Ruben, nine. All had preservers and were preparing to jump. "We'll all go over together," she said. "And remember this; remember! If you get separated from us, meet us at the Roosevelt Hotel. Your Mom and Dad will be there."

Another woman, Mary Lione of Long Island City, had become separated from her husband and eldest son and was calling, "Anthony—Raymond!" But too many others, in the same predicament, were shouting also, so that names and voices became hopelessly confused. Mrs. Lione had her other son with her but did not want to jump without her husband. Finally, when a seaman came up to her and said, "Lady, you and your boy better get over," she cried, "I'm afraid to!"

"I'll take him with me." He bent down to the boy.

"Will you hold on to my back good and tight? What's your name?"

"Robert."

"How old are you?"

"Four."

"Will you hold on to me, Robert?"

When the boy nodded he lifted him on to his back, told Mrs. Lione to follow, and jumped. A stewardess saw him, put a lost child on her back, and did the same thing.

On other decks people were tying coats and jackets together and lowering children that way. Among these children were Benito Rueda, seven, and his younger brother, three. They were swept about for hours by the waves and finally carried onto the beach by the breakers. Benito was taken immediately to a hospital. The other child was dead.

On C deck, Charles Wright, a headwaiter, had about twenty or thirty passengers in tow. Earlier he had assembled them amidships, told them to hold hands, and proceeded to lead them aft in the hope of getting them to the boat deck via the crew's stairway. By that time the fire had moved above them, however, so they never did get to the boats.

The ship's carpenter, Johnson, came by with a line and he and Charles Wright put it over the side. Passengers were apparently more afraid of the thirty-foot jump than of the water itself, for once the rope was made fast, they wasted no time in climbing down. Even the elderly lady who had been bewildered in the corridor earlier decided to try it. She got caught in the line part of the way down, however, and Johnson had to climb down with a knife in his teeth and cut her loose.

Now the shortened line no longer reached the water, so Mr. and Mrs. Thorpe Aschoff, on their wedding trip, got up on the rail, held hands, and jumped in together. A strong swimmer, Mr. Aschoff had given his preserver to a woman a short while before, which meant that he had a seven-mile swim ahead of him and a wife who would need his assistance all the way.

At least five other couples followed the Aschoffs' example. Mr. and Mrs. Abraham Cohen of Hartford, Connecticut, were among them, Dr. and Mrs. Jules Blondeau of Philadelphia, and Frieda and Alexander McArthur. Mr. McArthur, forty-two, was an excellent swimmer, but his wife could barely tread water. The Cohens were even worse off, with only one preserver between them and Mrs. Cohen able to swim no more than a few strokes. But they were young and in excellent physical condition. Mr. Cohen had played on the 1924-25 Dartmouth football team.

Lloyd Barnstead, a New York accountant, saw a life ring in the water shortly after he and his wife had jumped from deck. He swam to it, towed it back to where his wife was floating, and slipped it over her head. But they were afraid the ship might explode and suck them under, so they changed their minds, held the ring out in front of them and started kicking.

It was at about this time that John Kempf, the New York fireman, found himself surrounded in the water by six women, one of whom, calmly paddling, shocked and delighted him with the remark, "Well, we're all in the same boat, so let's make the best of it."

Kempf would never again believe movies that depicted women screaming through moments of crisis. "The women were calmer than the men," he said. "They would have been smoking cigarettes in the water if they could have."

It was perhaps this calmness or low-keyed excitement on the part of the six women around him that prompted Kempf to jam his chin peremptorily above a breaking wave and say, "Get away from the ship. There are gallons and gallons of oil in there."

"Are you an officer, mister?" one of the women asked.

Kempf, who admitted afterwards that he had a great love for the uniforms one sees at ships' dances, could not resist answering in the affirmative. "It was to increase their morale and give a little added confidence," he said.

Not everybody would jump from the ship, however. Rafael Mestre, the Cuban passenger who had made a bargain with himself to jump if Mrs. Phelps did, was still standing on the B-deck rail, unable to get up courage because of the height.

"Get over!" "Jump!" "Push him, somebody!" People behind him began shouting.

Mestre had hold of the scupper above on A deck, and as his feet were knocked from under him, he got another grip and, with legs dangling over the water and the shouts of the crowd in his ears, managed to pull himself up the outside rail to the high poop on "A." He had actually hindered himself by climbing, for he was now higher above the water; and up here, where the wind ran free, the flames were closer. He saw a woman weeping because she had no preserver and, showing none of the hesitation he'd shown toward jumping, took his preserver off and gave it to her.

"You jump now, yes?" Mestre said. He kept nodding in an effort to get her to nod, for some woman behind them had begun to scream and Mestre could not shake off the idea that he, in particular, was expected to save her. He finally cradled this woman in his arms, lifted her over the rail and, holding her as far out as possible so she wouldn't hit the fishplates on the way down, let go.

The woman found her voice on the way down, and luckily landed on the small of her back. "God bless you!" she cried on coming to the surface, "God bless you!" whereupon Mestre, giving himself up to death, started into the superstructure to save the trapped and screaming woman. He managed to get to one smoking cabin, then another, but could find no one and could no longer even hear the screams. Just then he tripped over something and, thinking it was the woman, grabbed and tussled with it for several seconds before realizing it was too light to be a woman. He felt the canvas skin, the straps and arm holes, and found a new greed for life. Running out on deck, he tied the preserver on and went bucketing into the water.

He went way under and stayed under, he thought, for a long time. But once on the surface, shocked to life by the water and convinced that the preserver would keep him afloat, he felt new again. He saw a rope hanging over the side of the ship and grabbed it, looking upward along the blistered wall of steel and then around again at the dark and heavily rolling seas. There was a friend of his in a lifebelt floating by, Rosario Comacho. Mestre was suddenly happy.

"Hello, Rosario, how are you?"

"Where am I?"

"You are in water."

"I think I am on boat."

"You are not; you are in water. Keep it up."

This, while she floated away and someone slid down the rope on top of Mestre, making him let go.

He began to drift under the secret part of the ship where the propellers were. The hull was all rounded back here like the world and he was outside it, outside the world. The propellers were stopped, one blade on the portside half showing, the one on the starboard straight up in the air like a twisted fin. He could have held on to one of the blades but was afraid to, thinking that if the propeller turned . . . He just didn't want to touch it. The blades, gleaming wet and sharp-looking, seemed to belong to the sea, not to the trip up from Cuba at all. They kept slipping into the water and out again, in and out, as the stern pawed the ocean that it lived with and knew so well.

His thoughts had been of people along the side of the ship; back here he thought of the scavenger sniff of sharks making their rounds of an anchorage in the night. He caught the fear in his throat and wanted to reach up, but the stern was smoothly closed to him. He kicked and started off after his friend, Rosario Comacho. "Rosario," he called with his back to the bad place, "Rosario! Are you there—somewhere?"

14

Sometime after 4:00 A.M., a man named Chalfont, a boat acquaintance of young Phelps (they had played bridge earlier that evening), noticed Phelps on C deck without a preserver and suggested that they go over together and that Phelps cling to him.

"He implored me to go over with him and use his belt," Phelps said, "but I couldn't do that. I knew it wouldn't be enough for the two of us."

A half hour had passed since his parents had abandoned ship. "I thought of them out in that blackness and wondered if they were clinging to each other." Finally he stripped his clothes off and slid down one of the warping cables that someone had lowered from deck.

"When I got into the water I could see another rope dangling about twenty feet away. I made for that. A wave lifted me and threw me within arm's reach of it. That was sheer luck."

For hours Phelps was pounded against the *Castle* by the waves, pelted by falling bits of hot metal, wood and splashes of paint, but he would not let go of the rope. He saw a lifeboat, "apparently manned by some of the ship's crew, pass through the water where men and women were yelling and screaming and imploring to be taken in, but the crewmen in the boat did not stop to pick anyone up. There seemed to be only about eight or nine men in that boat.

"Later I saw another lifeboat go through those people, making no effort to help or take anyone aboard. Some of the men in the boat seemed to be having difficulty with the oars and some of them seemed to be clinging to the seats. People in the water tried to clutch at the gunwales, but they all seemed to miss and the boat drifted on."

The crewmen of this second boat claimed later that it was impossible to handle the oars properly in such a high sea, and that the boat, in the contrary way of lifeboats riding waves, kept sliding away from outstretched hands and then sweeping away altogether.

There was one passenger in this second boat, a man named Matthew McElheny who, though not rowing himself, kept urging the seamen at oars to exert every effort to save the women and children in the water. The seamen tried their best to do McElheny's bidding, though they were so sick from the smoke that they kept vomiting over themselves as they rowed. "They tried to stay in the vicinity of the ship for over an hour," McElheny said later, "but were half choked and sick from fighting the fire."

A little later, Phelps himself was "too far gone to help" several women struggling toward the knotted monkey lines hanging from the empty davits amidships. "They held on for brief periods before the waves tore them away into the dark. I had to watch those women drop off one by one and float off and hear their desperate and familiar voices pleading. I'd met them and danced with them," he said.

The fact remains that of the first ninety-eight people to escape in lifeboats, ninety-two were members of the crew. Passengers trapped at the stern or struggling in the water cried for help as the waves swept these almost empty boats shoreward, and later, those who lived through the experience expressed their grievances openly.

It was never explained why the sea anchors in these lifeboats were not used. A sea anchor is a cone-shaped affair, usually of canvas stretched on a frame and hung over the bow of a lifeboat in such a way as to resist motion in the water the way a parachute does in the air. The use of these sea anchors by the seamen in the boats around the *Morro Castle* would have kept the boats from drifting so rapidly away from the ship and enabled passengers struggling in the water to swim close enough to be hauled in. The failure to use them is perhaps explained by the fact that those in the lifeboats were afraid of the ship blowing up.

"Everyone seemed panic-stricken and the crew did nothing as far as I could see to help passengers out," Miss Sydney Folkman of New York City said. "The passengers had to do everything for themselves."

"Officers and stewards were simply splendid," Lewis Perrone said, "but ordinary seamen went over the side at the first opportunity."

"I saw fifty to sixty seamen, not only with preservers," David Schneider said, "but with life rings around themselves as well. I mean the preservers weren't enough for them." (There were not fifty to sixty but exactly eighteen life rings on the ship.)

"I did not see any officer or sailor even to ask what had happened," Nathan Feinberg, a passenger, said. "I and everyone else aboard learned about the fire from fellow passengers. I felt the crew had been negligent in not giving the alarm and getting us up before we woke of our own accord."

Able-bodied Seaman Morris Weisberger had an explanation for this. "When the crew was called, the situation had already become critical. The call came too late. Then there was no direction as to 'what to do.' So everyone did what he thought should be done."

The crew claimed that the passengers could have reached the lifeboats if they had not been afraid to walk forward against the wind and smoke. Sailors said that they urged passengers to do this, but were unheeded because the passengers either decided it was poor advice or refused to realize the seriousness of the situation until it was too late. Antonio Georgio, an oiler who left in number three boat with Quartermaster Hoffman, a sailor named Bernhardt, a bellboy, and the man who worked on the ice machine, said that there were no passengers in the vicinity of their boat except one girl. When Georgio tried to grab this girl and get her into the boat, she was so frightened of him (he had brilliant tattoo marks on both arms) that she ran away and jumped overboard.

Stewardess Sarah Kirby, who had spent a lifetime at sea and was making her last trip aboard the *Morro Castle,* said, "There were two old ladies who clung to me on deck. I held on to them as long as I could.

Women were screaming, men were running. I saw some of our crewmen take off their life belts and put them on passengers. Then I don't know what happened. We were separated by the rush of people and the flames drove into us."

"The crewmen were fine," Regina Gilligan, a passenger, said. "The officers were calm and tried to keep the crowd from getting panicky. They succeeded, too. They kept everybody in tow and gave us all a lot of confidence. There was no panic at any time. We knew the captain had died a few hours before, but we all trusted the remaining officers. And the crew fought the fire up to the very last minute."

"The members of the crew knew how to swim and they weren't afraid to jump," Ivan Freeman said. "A sailor will jump from a high deck with a life preserver on because he knows that he'll come up to the top and be all right. Lots of the women were afraid to jump and put it off until the last minute, and by that time they were half full of smoke and they were not in a physical condition to stay alive when they got in the water."

There was no deficiency of life-saving equipment on the *Morro Castle*. On the contrary, the dozen 30-foot steel lifeboats were capable of carrying 816 people, or 300 more than were aboard the ship at the time of the fire. In addition, there were 12 balsa-wood floats capable of supporting 204 persons in the water, 18 life buoys attached to railings along the upper decks, and 851 life preservers, 78 of which were especially designed for the use of children. But many people at the stern, though in some cases as a result of their own negligence, were without preservers, and only one balsa-wood float ever did reach the water. Indeed, counting all the life-saving equipment—lifeboats, floats, buoys and preservers— 1,900 people might have been saved, or approximately four times as many as were on the ship.

But life-saving equipment on a ship, no matter how plentiful or up-to-date, is dependent upon the caliber and attitude of the men assigned to put it into operation during a crisis. The Ward Line's reputation for niggardliness was well known in 1934 by seamen congregating along South Street in New York. Those who did sign on a Ward Line ship were, therefore, often the least able; and not only that, they had no loyalty to the company for the reason that neither the line nor the passengers showed any interest in their problems.

It is doubtful whether any of the passengers who condemned the self-interest of seamen during the fire had taken the trouble during the voyage to find out what their monthly salary was. Able seamen on the *Morro Castle* received the minimum wage of $50 a month. Oilers received $30 less than their minimum, or $60 a month. Ordinary seamen received $35 a month, quartermasters $55, firemen $52, and stewards and stewardesses (who also received tips) $40. Chief Radio Operator Rogers was listed on the company's pay sheets as making $120 a month, while Acting Captain Warms was listed as making only $180.

Surely in 1934, when this country was in its worst depression, there was something anachronistic about the attitude of passengers who expected seamen to be ethical to the point of death when the company hiring them wasn't even ethical to the point of wages. Right up to the outbreak of the fire, when suddenly "the code of the sea" called for these seamen to lay down their lives if necessary, they were virtually invisible, men who, if they made too much noise during a fire-and-boat drill or ran to their stations with anything like the energy suggestive of the real thing, were reported by passengers to the captain for disturbing what the Ward Line itself had advertised as a "pleasure cruise."

William O'Sullivan, the deck storekeeper, said that only two stations responded to the regular weekly fire drills, "because we didn't want to disturb the passengers."

Captain Wilmott was responsible for this condition, not Chief Officer Warms. It was Wilmott who dined with the passengers and who knew that the paying out of fire hose, the sudden show of preservers and the swinging out of boats (required by law once a week), often frightened his passengers to the point where they could no longer enjoy the ship's cuisine.

People from the central part of the United States especially, more used to rivers and ferries than to oceans and ships, resent these reminders of danger and the need to be prepared for it. One steward aboard the *Morro Castle* actually spoke of the "glaring look" a passenger gave him when he offered to show the passenger how to adjust his life preserver. "That will do," the passenger said, with such venom that the steward, whose livelihood depended on tips, decided never to make the offer again.

The same passenger no doubt preferred the following advertising circular he'd picked up at the Ward Line office where he'd bought his ticket:

The Morro Castle *and* Oriente *are protected throughout with proven safety devices of the latest type, including radio sending and receiving sets, radio direction finders, automatic electric fire alarms, automatically operated fire doors, electrically controlled bulkhead doors, automatic detecting and chemical fire-extinguishing systems, Fathometers, Watchman's clock system, a complete Sperry Gyroscope system, including automatic steering, powerful fog siren, searchlight, helm indicators, Jachometers, and embody structural safeguards of an advanced nature which contribute toward making these vessels the safest afloat.*

The passengers who prefer and expect to be saved "automatically" are usually the ones whose ethical standards are shocked if, during a crisis, a seaman or steward doesn't materialize in time to lay down his life in their behalf. The "code" that calls for such selflessness on a seaman's part goes back to a time when class distinctions made unequal human sacrifice at least a working hypothesis. Such class distinctions no longer exist, at least not in any generally accepted sense, and neither does the code except in the minds of those still in a position to benefit from it.

"Equality" has set in, so that today, despite the fact that an American seaman works under excellent conditions, receives very good wages and is fed the best of food (union contracts call for meat twice a day, not counting the bacon at breakfast), a passenger would be foolhardy indeed to expect him to put anyone else's life before his own. There will always be the exceptions like Arthur Stamper and Trygue Johnson, but perhaps even that is wishful thinking.

"Seamen belong to their own times," wrote William McFee shortly after the *Morro Castle* disaster. "They reflect pretty accurately the ethics and the mores of their patrons."

15

"You never heard such praying in all your life," David Schneider, the exporter of textiles, said of those who refused to abandon ship. The older women especially made a chapel of every dark corner and recess at the stern. They huddled together and prayed aloud; some knelt erect while others bent over like Mohammedans. All seemed addicted rather than devoted to God. Yet, since without prayers to say they might have lost their minds, their prayers were answered.

Then Father Egan of St. Mary's Church in the Bronx appeared with Henry Stamm, the switchboard operator, who had agreed to help him reach those hopelessly burned but still alive. The right side of Father Egan's face had been burned, and now, out on deck and aft of the flaming superstructure, they continued their quiet pilgrimage. Stamm had a wet rag with which he kept dabbing Father Egan's face, and there was something in his attempt to be gentle that reminded several survivors of the relationship between altar boy and priest. Father Egan accepted the small mercy, sometimes while raising his hand in benediction, in a way that made one almost believe again in the princeliness of man. As one survivor put it: "They were like dwellings in the past, these corners of the ship as Father Egan came to them. They were free of both doubt and skepticism."

One pathetic woman, though, seemed to be trying to bridge the gap between faith and reason. She had been most devout, making the sign of the cross above her head; but with Father Egan gone to comfort others, she kept interrupting her prayers to look at the fire. She alternated so often between praying and looking that it was impossible to tell whether she was asking God for deliverance from the fire or merely keeping Him informed of its development.

Meanwhile the cruise director shouted up and down the decks, "Get your children over! Please hurry. Jump!"

But when parents put their children on the rail, they looked down at the water and hesitated. Finally, Lewis

Perrone and John Kent, looking like officers in their white mess jackets, fought their way through the crowd to the rail, made sure that each child had a preserver, and began pushing them over. They succeeded in getting about twenty over this way, and it was their determination, plus the sudden burst of flame through the salon partition, that started the mass abandonment of the ship.

"Why weren't the fire doors at the stern closed? I'll probably be thinking about that all my life," the ship's carpenter, Trygue Johnson, said later. "But there were people behind those doors and I didn't want to shut them out. Once closed, the doors would have trapped the people behind them."

Parents scrambled over the railings after their children and then everybody began going over, "like apples dumped from a barrel," as one survivor put it.

"One girl took her slippers off and jumped," Night Watchman Arthur Pender said. "Her toes caught in the railing; her clothes burst into flames. I couldn't see any way to help her. I kicked her. She slipped free and fell into the water, her body a flaming torch."

A passenger, George Whitlock, began begging Pender to save his wife, a cripple. Pender got some rope, broke down a door and made a stretcher of it. He and the husband then lowered the crippled woman into the water, whereupon the husband, thanking Pender, scaled the rail and jumped. Both Whitlock and his wife were saved, and later Whitlock visited Pender in the hospital to thank him again.

Young Phelps, hanging on to his rope, could hear the roar as the flames broke through. Then came "a rain of people, a hundred or more, over the side of the ship to escape the suddenly released flames. They hit one another in their descent; many sank out of sight immediately."

Many, on coming back to the surface, began reaching back toward the ship. They might have risen from another world to board her, for she was no longer sumptuous and gay and studded with electric lights, but a floating furnace round which heads bobbed in the firelight. Those without preservers kept reaching toward her anyway, preferring, at the last moment, a different death than the one fate was dealing them.

Many in the water were amazed to see human forms amidships, dancing one minute behind a flame, the next minute in front of another. Most amazing of all was a man without a preserver, leaning over the rail on the portside of the superstructure with a cigarette in his mouth. His hunched shoulders and head gave him the aspect of a man gazing down matter-of-factly on a dock, at longshoremen heaving crates into a cargo net. The man was immense in his composure with the fire right behind him. There was so little suggestion of fear that people in the water later remembered wondering why they'd jumped. It never became clear who he was, but many survivors said they would never forget him.

Another man was not so much brave as practical. He wanted his wife to take a drink from his flask before they slid down a mooring cable into the water. "Here. Keep you warm. Calm you." He anticipated her distaste and bellowed, "Do as I tell you, for once!"

It was Scotch and the peaty taste made her wince. "The smoke's gotten into it."

"That's what you think," he said. "Come on."

Still on C deck, and about to be called on to make an almost impossible decision, was Dr. S. Joseph Bregstein. His son, Mervin, equipped with a child's preserver, was with him. The doctor had no preserver and could not swim, but he saw clearly that in a matter of minutes his choice would be to burn to death or drown.

Just outside the rail where Bregstein and his son stood were two young women from Shrewsbury, Massachusetts, Gladys and Ethel Knight, both excellent swimmers. The straps of their preservers had become entangled and they had asked Dr. Bregstein to untangle them before they jumped. Gladys Knight took a young girl over the rail with her and started the seven-mile swim to shore with the girl. Suddenly Ethel Knight began begging the doctor to let her take his son. "I can help to hold him up," she said.

Dr. Bregstein saw the rescue ships on the horizon and glanced behind him. If he refused Ethel's request, his son would have to go overboard anyway, and alone, before the rescue ships arrived. If he accepted, Ethel might be able to keep his head above the waves.

The flames were so close now that sparks and embers were burning holes in his clothing; the heat behind him was intense. He nodded to Ethel and, kissing his boy, lifted him over to her. There was a second's hesitation, then as Ethel let go with the boy in her arms, the impulse to protect him to the very end sent the doctor scrambling over the rail himself. He wanted to jump but instead, with tears in his eyes and anguish in his heart, hung there.

What happened then might have deprived a lesser man of his sanity. Someone still on the ship, and at a lower level, grabbed Dr. Bregstein by the legs and said, "Come on, I'll pull you in." It was Jim Hassall, another passenger, who thereupon pulled the doctor in on D deck—a deck the doctor had not known existed, the one to which Third Engineer Arthur Stamper had escaped from the engine room. The whole black gang was there, having used the same escape route five minutes ahead of Stamper, as well as about fifty more passengers who had been led down from C by Second Engineer Aubrey Russell and Cruise Director Robert Smith. D deck was still relatively free of flames, not only because the fire had originated on a higher level, but because Stamper and his men had the necessary water pressure to keep the flames at bay.

Bregstein leaned over the rail and called, "Mervin! Ethel!" but they had drifted off in the black water and he heard nothing but the foamy swish against the ship. And though Ethel Knight did her utmost to keep the boy's head above the onrushing seas, she became unconscious after about an hour and the boy was lost. Meanwhile Dr. Bregstein was able to remain aboard until the rescue ships arrived.

Fire at Sea

16

A twenty-six-foot surfboat from the Coast Guard Station at Sea Girt, New Jersey, was the first rescue boat to arrive on the scene. The skipper and four coastguardmen had set out for the "ball of flame" before receiving the *Morro Castle*'s S O S, and now as Warren R. Moulton, at the engine controls, stopped the boat in the flame-lit waters by the ship, he saw what he knew even then he would never forget.

In a letter to his sister about this experience, which *The New Republic* later published, Moulton wrote: "The ocean was fairly lit up by the light of the burning ship, and the water was simply alive with screaming men and women. We stopped, and it very nearly spelled the end of us and a great many others, for so many grabbed the boat at once that we were nearly capsized and sunk. I do not know how many minutes we stopped, but certainly not more than five, and I heard the Skipper bellowing at me to go ahead on her. I got her under way and for the next half mile there was a fight on that I will never forget. Every sea broke over us, washing us from stem to stern. The crew did all they could to keep others off, and prevent our running over someone in the water; the Skipper was at the tiller, I at the engine controls. The water was so deep that my hands on the gas throttle were covered. All around, ahead, on each side and stern, were men and women, all excited, a few with their hands stretched out to us, calling for help; and we, already overloaded, unable to help at all. The rain beat down, the spray flew, and the way those upturned faces looked as they rose on the crest of a wave with the firelight flickering on them was awful."

Charles Menken, a New York City policeman, had just found his wife in the water when the surfboat bounded up on a heave of sea. He managed to get hold of the boat before it passed and cried, "For God's sake, take the women!" He had been knocked unconscious by someone falling from the ship on top of him, but he had his wits about him now. When they pulled his wife aboard, he said he'd hold on, so in desperation they pulled him aboard, too.

The skipper then headed east in the hope that rescue vessels would soon be arriving from seaward of the burning ship. He could then unload his survivors and go back for more. Moulton managed to crowd a little more speed on, and soon the people in the water were left behind.

Terror seized them as the surfboat passed by. They fought, exhausted, until the waves rolled over them, despite their preservers.

A girl about eleven swam up to Charles Wright, the headwaiter, and tried to support herself on his life belt. "I knew who she was, one of the Saenz children, but I didn't know if it was Caina or Martha. I told her to put her arm around my neck and she did. Her face was badly burned.

"After a long time she seemed to be getting weaker. She had not even whimpered, but I noticed that after waves went over us she seemed to have more and more difficulty spitting the water out. I began to hold her up as much as I could, though I thought the waves going over us would be cool to her burned face . . .

"She became unconscious and I held on until I was sure she was dead. During that time another woman, about forty, hung on to my life belt. That put a pretty good strain on it, so I grabbed an oar that floated by to help keep us up.

"We kept meeting people in the water. I spoke to a lot of them I knew. One was a young woman in a red woolen bathing suit. She had put it on to swim ashore in."

Adele and Ed Brady were in the water for hours when Mr. Brady's strength became exhausted. Despite having been ill, and not yet fully recovered, he insisted on helping his wife. There was something benign about his exhaustion, for after a while he said, "Adele, I don't think I can make it, but I don't mind. I'm very tired."

"A boat will be along any minute!" his wife said. *"Please* stay with me!"

Brady removed more of his clothes between breaths and nauseating gulps of salt water, but the deeps pulled at him and he began reaching upward, no longer forward. At times only his hair floated, then he would force his mouth up high enough to nibble air. Finally he reached inside his jacket, took out his wallet, and gave it to his wife. Mrs. Brady, who was holding on to him, watched his last bit of strength leave him as he bunched himself together, pushed her away and with the admonition, "Save yourself," disappeared.

Mr. and Mrs. Charles Filster, in the same predicament, clung to the body of a dead passenger to buoy themselves in the water, until Mr. Filster was swept away by a wave and lost.

There is nothing quite so alien as the sea after a ship has been abandoned. As one young writer who jumped in without a preserver put it: "The water's thievery of your body's heat, the false testimony of the wind, the straining of your eyes until you 'see' rescue boats that aren't there, the pulsation from belief to disbelief in your imminent non-existence—all make one long hell of such a night."

17

In the Marine Vista Room of the Belmar, New Jersey, Fishing Club, a pine and glass structure perched high above surf, dunes and poison ivy, five night owls were playing cards. Suddenly the night watchman ran in, his arms waving frantically toward the sea.

"There's something the matter out there. It can't be the sun coming up this early. Something's the matter!"

Mrs. Benjamin Farrier, one of the players, glanced at her watch. "Of course not. It isn't four o'clock."

The five players went to the glass wall looking east to the Atlantic, and "the light on the water kept getting more and more brilliant," Mrs. Farrier said. "We knew it must be a big ship on fire. It was the most awful and wonderful sight I have ever seen, that light spreading over the sea.

"Somebody said it was about six miles out. We telephoned the Coast Guard Station at Shark River, near Avon. They said yes, they had had radio messages and the ship was the *Morro Castle*.

"It rained very hard from then on, but that did not quench the flames. We could not make out the ship, but only that terrible light blazing out on the ocean."

More boats from the Jersey shore would almost certainly have reached the burning ship were it not for the violence of the storm. At least forty pleasure craft off Brielle had been compelled to make for shore when the storm grew violent about 1 A.M. Had the water been calm enough for them to remain at anchor, their captains would have seen the flaming ship and made for it. Hundreds of smaller vessels that could have picked up ten times as many people as were struggling in the water around the ship were warped to docks less than ten miles away because of the storm.

At Blodgett's Landing at Point Pleasant, fishermen were lying around the wharf because it was too rough to fish. The masts of their fishing boats swayed above them as they "chewed the fat" about a large ship burning off the coast. They knew about it from a radio announcement, but did nothing because, according to the announcer, "All hands had been saved."

These fishermen at Blodgett's Landing had bitter things to say about the Coast Guard the next day for allowing that erroneous report to pass uncorrected, but another fisherman, Captain Jimmy Bogen, whose boat, the *Paramount,* was tied up just inside the Manasquan Inlet, had the presence of mind to call and ask the Coast Guard if he could be of any assistance.

"You sure can," he was told. "Go on out there as fast as you can."

Twenty-six-year-old Captain Jimmy, "the youngest skipper on the coast," whose father owned the boat and whose kid brother was a member of the crew, immediately began calling along the dock for the most experienced hands available. Besides his father and brother, Bogen mustered an all-captain crew from other Manasquan fishing boats. Captain William Fuhrman jumped up to go, and so did Captains Knute Lovegren, Charles Gifford, Thomas McDowell and Clayton Weller. They were no sooner aboard than Captain Jimmy, at the wheel, headed offshore and right for the burning *Castle.* The 30-gross-ton *Paramount,* 54 feet long, 5 feet high at the stern and with an especially wide beam for taking fishing parties out to deep water, was more than equal to the storm that was raging, and these were professionals who knew their waters, how to handle a boat, and the meaning of the word "distress."

Before they got near the ship they took people out of the water from all sides. "We didn't bother with bodies," Jimmy said. "We only picked up live ones. They were all over. If they had on life preservers, we got them with grappling hooks, but otherwise we had to jockey the boat alongside and grab them."

And though all six captains were intent and almost brutally efficient at their task, though they appreciated the desperation of those screaming for help in the water and did everything in their power to get to them in time, they could not help making mental notes of the curlers in a woman's hair, the polka dots in a man's pajamas, a missing sock, a torn negligee, a hearing aid in someone's ear, a diamond ring on a bloody finger and the strange, detaining poignancy of an operation scar on a fat man's belly. It was as if what mattered, what they were really struggling to haul in and save, were not this or that human being but the appurtenances of humanity itself.

When they came to Frieda and Alexander McArthur, one of the couples who had jumped hand in hand from the ship, Mr. McArthur was dead from the exertion of trying to keep his wife's head above the surface. When Jim Bogen shouted down to her to let her husband go

("We can't take dead persons"), Mrs. McArthur refused. She had hold of a rope from the *Paramount* with one hand but managed to keep hold of her husband's life-belt with the other. They kept trying to convince her to let her husband go, but she held on and shook her head, weeping up at them through the mist and spray. Her husband represented the tragedy too vividly to be left behind.

"Finally she looked around and saw all the screaming people in the water who needed our help," Jimmy said. "After that she released her hold and we lifted her aboard."

One thing that struck Jim Bogen especially was "the way families would stick together. I remember a wife and daughter holding up the old man and the old man was dead. We couldn't waste time with him. We made them let go of him and we hauled them in."

He was referring to Doris and Mr. and Mrs. Wacker, the three who had put their life preservers on backwards and abandoned ship together. Doris had alternated between her father and mother in the water, trying to relieve them both as all three looked in vain for rescue boats.

"My father had sinus trouble and it made it very difficult for him to breathe in the water. In the rough seas the waves kept washing over us even though I kept trying to keep them both up. Finally father said, 'Let me go. I've had enough.' I couldn't do that, but he was soon unconscious, and then he died."

The *Paramount* then came upon the New York City fireman, John Kempf, and the six women. The ladies had banded together around their "ship's officer," who had been both buoyed by their esteem and helpfully talkative throughout their vigil for a rescue boat. Over the radio a few days later, John Kempf said, "I hope the skipper of the *Paramount* is listening in. If it was in my power, I'd buy him the *Leviathan* and put him in charge."

He also had high praise for the six women, as well as a continuing interest in them, for during the same investigation by the Steamboat Inspectors in the Custom House in New York (the first famous inquiry broadcast in American history), he said, "I hope the redheaded girl and all the other girls and those I met on shipboard will remember me and the pleasant times we had and send me some postal cards." Whereupon he pressed his lips to the microphone and kept them there until one of the investigators pulled it away from him.

At one point during the *Paramount*'s rescue operations, John Bogen, Sr. was pulled overboard by an exceptionally heavy woman he was trying to save. He hit his chin against the bulwark as he tumbled over and was knocked unconscious. But he never let go of the woman, and when Captains Lovegren and Fuhrman jumped overboard to help, they found Bogen and the woman still together. They got Bogen aboard but the woman, a Cuban Mae West, defied the best efforts of the six captains to lift her on deck. They finally had to use a rope hoist from high up on the mast, the kind used for raising fish-laden nets out of the sea.

What happened then captured the attention of everybody aboard the *Paramount*. The three Bogens rescued a couple who lived on the very same block with them in Jersey City. Mr. and Mrs. Paul Lemprecht, married only a week, had chosen the *Morro Castle* for their wedding cruise. They were not only friends and neighbors of the Bogens, they had often fished off the Jersey shore from the *Paramount*'s deck. When Mrs. Lemprecht was lifted aboard, she threw her arms around Jimmy and cried, "Thank God!"

"We rescued a girl reporter who was a honey," Jimmy said. " 'Pick up the others first,' she told us. Her only request was that she be allowed to keep her preserver for a souvenir."

Captain Jimmy admired her looks, her smile, her courage—and told her so. She liked Jimmy herself, but limited her reply.

"Well, I'm a reporter," she said.

18

Many hours later a lone plane came boring eastward over the water. It was an army plane, but survivors struggling in the heavy seas said that when they first looked up and saw it, they were so suddenly filled with courage that they thought of Charles Lindbergh. The famous Englewood kidnaping had revived the colonel's name, but that wasn't why, the survivors said, they thought of Lindbergh. It was rather the sight of the plane itself, the way it came out from land to negotiate the oblivion of that dawn-lit sea.

"I saw an army plane circling overhead," Dr. Phelps

said, "and I waved at the man in it and he waved at me. I said to my wife, 'Katherine, he surely will help us.'"

After the Phelpses had had their mattress sunk from under them in the vicinity of the blazing ship, they had found a pole which turned out to be an oar with the blade burned off.

"I thought it would at least help to keep us together," the doctor said. "Later we picked up another pole, an oar with the blade burned away like the first one . . . so we kept swimming with our little pieces of wood."

The Phelpses didn't know it, but the man waving to them from the plane was Governor A. Harry Moore of New Jersey. On being informed of the disaster, he hurried to the National Guard campgrounds, donned a pneumatic life belt and, disregarding the advice of army officers who did not want the governor to go up on such a stormy morning, strapped himself in the first available plane. The pilot, Captain John A. Carr of the 44th Aviation Division, took off and headed for the waters off Sea Girt.

It was an open-cockpit military plane, and the governor, leaning out as the plane dipped and banked over the water, would see a victim and tell the pilot to circle the spot. The governor would then wave a red flag, both to let the person know he'd been discovered, and to point him out to whatever small vessel happened to be plying the waters in that vicinity. From his vantage point, the governor could see how close a rescue boat was to some victim in a way that those aboard the rescue boat could not.

"Gouv, I hear a noise!" Mrs. Phelps said soon after the plane had circled them and left. "Look, there's a launch!"

"The launch circled round," the doctor said, "stopping about thirty feet to the windward and threw us a rope, which I grabbed and passed around my wife. We discarded our beloved oars and they pulled us aboard."

Meanwhile their son, Phelps, Jr., was still clinging to the rope hanging from the stern of the *Morro Castle*. When finally he was picked off, by a boat from the *City of Savannah,* he was so exhausted that he fell into a faint in the bottom of the boat. An oiler from the *Morro Castle,* named Reginald Roberts, who had been hauled from the water into the same boat, criticized young Phelps for this.

"Young Phelps at no time tried to man an oar and I believe he could have. The way he seemed after we got to the *City of Savannah,* he was no more exhausted than any of the other men who pulled oars."

Phelps, Jr., vehemently disagreed with Roberts: "I had clung to the rope six hours when the lifeboat came and rescued me. I was stark naked when they lifted me out, and I lost consciousness as soon as I was in the boat—it might have been a minute or an hour—

but we were not yet back to the freighter when I regained my senses.

"The wind was blowing a gale and I was numb with cold, so the first thing I did was climb into the nearest seat—I had been lying in the bottom—and grab an oar. Though I was exhausted from hanging on to the rope for six hours, I rowed all the way back to the *City of Savannah*. I sat next to George Brill, a sailor from the freighter, and remember joking with him about my feeble efforts. I was shivering and exhausted, but I rowed for all I was worth because I thought the exertion would restore my circulation.

"Roberts's saying I didn't row is entirely unfair. I did row all the way back to the ship. . . . I'm sure he must have confused me with someone else. The lifeboat was not undermanned. So far as I could see, every oar was in use. In fact, I at first hunted for an extra oar and then had to take hold of Brill's oar and work with him. The boat was handled magnificently. I can't praise its crew enough. They displayed the best seamanship I've ever seen. They all pulled together as if they had rowed in a rough sea every day of their lives."

Captain Jimmy Bogen of the *Paramount* didn't know that the man in the plane was the Governor of New Jersey either, but he certainly appreciated the airborne assistance. "A United States Army plane flew over and did the spotting for us, pointing to where the passengers were foundering in the water. We picked them up right and left."

Governor Moore said, "It was a sight I shall never forget. One man in particular impressed me with the thin line that may be drawn between life and death. He was struggling feebly, partly submerged, when he heard our plane and looked upward. I waved to him. A small boat was passing not twenty feet away, but could not see him because of the high waves that obscured their view. I spotted him for them and saw him safely taken aboard."

Meanwhile, the *Andrea S. Luckenback* had appeared on the scene with her blinker asking the men on the bow of the *Morro Castle* a seemingly foolish and un-necessary question: "Do you need assistance?"

In view of the ancient salvage law of the sea, however, according to which the salvager has a lien on the dis-abled vessel, it was a fitting and proper question. For though no regular schedule of charges goes with the salvage law itself, the courts which fix the amount in each case are very generous toward the salvager on the assumption that any humanitarian impulse like racing to a vessel in distress is that much more unfettered when it also involves financial gain.

Acting Captain Warms put a flashlight in Rogers's

hand and told him to send: "Yes, immediately, five hundred and forty passengers."

The *Luckenback* answered, "Will send boats," whereupon Rogers, more or less in passing ("It was just one of those things you do"), threw back, "Okay."

While this blinker conversation proceeded, the Coast Guard surfboat was drawing up to the *Luckenback* to unload the survivors she had picked up earlier in the dark.

"I looked at our cargo for the first time," Warren R. Moulton wrote in his letter to his sister. "Women back of me in the stern were piled three deep, men and women over the engine box, cordwood fashion, all alive. Just how many there were I do not know, for we had our hands full to get them aboard the ship and keep our boat from being smashed alongside.

"As soon as the last passenger was off and aboard ship, our skipper went aboard to get the Master to move in closer to the *Morro Castle* so as to be more help to us. Later he did. We started back for another load. Before we got to the burning ship two more steamers had arrived and put out lifeboats; I do not know how many, but quite a few. Most of them were heavily loaded then, but a few were not, and these were either hauling people out of the water or doing all in their power to draw up to the stern of the *Morro Castle* where there must have been two hundred people crowded, either along the deck rail, in the water, or hanging by ropes over the stern. We stopped and loaded with women, all women, except three men who were just about gone, right along-side of us.

"Finally we ran over to the *City of Savannah* (a tanker) and put them off. Those fellows and the Captain really gave us wonderful help. The minute we were alongside they threw us a line both forward and aft to make fast to before the boat even lost headway. They opened one of their cargo ports and lowered ropes to tie around the women and men who could not climb the ladder."

One of the rescue ships Moulton referred to was the *Monarch of Bermuda,* which had come out of the mist and crossed the *Morro Castle*'s bow soon after the surf-boat had drawn up to the *Luckenback* with its first load of survivors.

This Furness Line ship was handled with magnificent seamanship, coming so close it almost touched the *Morro Castle*'s anchor chain. As she veered 'round to starboard, Warms cupped his hands and shouted, "Take them off aft. We're okay here."

A man by the pilothouse of the *Monarch* waved and the men on the *Castle* remembered seeing the propellers and reading the sign, "Quadruple Screws, Keep Clear," as she slid past. She shot all the way around the *Castle*'s bow again, never more than two hundred feet away from the burning ship; and though the rain was lashing and the sea heavy, Captain Francis maneuvered to within sixty feet and set up a lee calm for his lifeboats. There was no panic, and in each boat an officer stood with the tiller in his hand, under complete control of the seamen under him.

This *Monarch of Bermuda,* which was to be destroyed by fire in drydock thirteen years later, had sped to the scene from the moment the *Morro Castle*'s location had cracked through the air. On board they were all prepared, and by the purser's door on C deck was a sign which read:

> *An appeal. Apparel, ladies and gentlemen, is urgently needed for the survivors of the* Morro Castle. *Any passenger having clothing for this cause to spare—would they kindly hand it to the purser's office on C deck? Thank you.*

When the two boats from the *Monarch* reached the bow of the *Morro Castle,* Warms shouted, "Take them off aft. We don't want to go." The boats went aft and one came forward again with some survivors in it. "We have two passengers you can have," Warms said, and the officer in the boat sang out, "Lower them away."

The crew had a Jacob's ladder but the woman, Mrs. Vosseler, insisted that her husband go first. The Jacob's ladder overhung the bow where the sides of the ship were concave, however, which meant that the ladder, made of rope except for metal rungs, dangled as freely as any ladder in a circus. Such a ladder is difficult for a young man to descend, and Dr. and Mrs. Vosseler were both over sixty.

Warms finally rigged up a kind of bo'sun's chair with a bowline and a life belt. "Mr. Freeman put the lady in and I lashed the gentleman. Then all hands got hold of a bight of rope and lowered them one at a time into the lifeboat. The lady fell into the arms of a Furness Line stewardess who was waiting in the boat to take charge of her."

Just then, out a porthole on the portside of the *Castle,* about a hundred feet from the forward housing, a woman began shouting, "Save me!"

Naked, she stuck her head and shoulders out, then her chest, then her waist, but her hips got stuck.

"I can't," she kept crying, "I can't!"

Warms told Freeman to take a heaving line, put one end of it around a preserver, and let the preserver drift aft in the water until it came to where the woman was struggling to free herself. "Hold it there so she can grab it when she falls."

While Freeman was carrying out this order, Warms, quickly judging where the woman's stateroom was located, shouted up along the side of the ship, "Get back in and put your *feet* out first." He was going to try to reach her from within; he just wanted to give her this advice beforehand in the event he failed or she succeeded in freeing herself without his help.

But when he started into the superstructure, it soon became obvious that the flames forcing her out the port were not limited to her cabin; they hopelessly separated him from her.

"I knew that if I could get through the linen locker and get upstairs I could get to her," Warms said. "I got through the thwartship alleyway and broke in the linen-locker door, but then the smoke started. I felt my way to the stairs, but there was no way of getting up. No way at all. All above me was fire."

Back on deck, he shouted again to the woman, "Jump *feet* first. Get your *feet* out."

"I'm—stuck," the woman kept screaming as the flames behind her drew closer. "I can't—I can't. Help me!"

From the waist up she was soaking wet from the rain racing across her body; from the waist down she was literally in an oven.

"I need a man to jump in," Warms said to the crew. "When this girl gets free and falls, somebody'll have to grab her."

The men on deck never for a moment doubted the woman's ability to free herself eventually. Having been

through the fire themselves and knowing at first hand
what the human body is capable of in its instinctive
repulsion from fire, they were not unfeeling so much
as practical.

The *Monarch* boats had started back, so somebody
had to go over the side and try to save the woman.
Rogers made several elaborate moves to go, but never
quite got around to it. Another man had his shoes off
and was down to his shorts before Rogers reached the
Jacob's ladder at the bow to climb down and go in for
her.

"I ran to the ladder to go in for her," Rogers said. "But
I had my shoes on, and when I stopped to kick them
off, someone shouted from the forepeak, "Don't jump,
Sparks; this man's going in."

"I don't remember Rogers saying he'd go in," Alagna
said. "I didn't see him go either, and I didn't hear anyone shout to him not to go."

It made a good story over the radio and in vaudeville
later, though, and Rogers again had proof, because he'd
kicked his shoes off into the water and had to go down
to the crew's quarters in the forepeak and see if he could
find another pair.

The man with shorts on jumped from deck just as the
screaming woman, giving one last final heave, freed
herself and fell into the water. The drop was over

twenty-five feet and she landed flat on her stomach and lay there floating with her arms stretched out, her face in the water.

Meanwhile the man who had jumped in to save her was himself beginning to drown. The sea was much rougher than he'd imagined; it threw him against the side of the ship until his whole left side was bleeding. He had not bothered with a preserver for fear it would retard his swimming, and now as the waves rolled over him he began to gasp and struggle and flail his arms for help. He had gone only 150 feet when he was forced to hold on to one of the lifeboat falls trailing in the water. He never reached the woman; she disappeared, and in about an hour another lifeboat took the man off.

By this time the Coast Guard surfboat was beginning to run out of gas. "We started to the leeward to take a look at the inlet to see if we could possibly get in," Warren R. Moulton wrote his sister. "When we were about two and a half miles from the *Morro Castle,* we saw two ship's lifeboats bob up away off on our starboard, but could not make out what they were doing, as it was raining so hard. They seemed to be drifting helplessly toward the breakers, about half a mile in shore. When we were [within] about a hundred yards of the first boat we saw a girl throw up her hands just a little away from us. We went to her and just as we got her on board, the rain slacked; as we rose on top of a sea, as far as we could see the ocean was dotted with both living and dead.

"We were but a few minutes in getting a load of the living, took the lifeboat in tow, and started for the *City of Savannah* two and a half miles to windward. The boat we had in tow was one of hers."

Captain Diehl of the *City of Savannah* said, "There was no doctor aboard, but we did what we could with blankets, hot coffee, tea and liquor when it was needed to make those we picked up comfortable. I gave somebody my hat and the only other suit I had on board, and all of my men divided up the same way. I don't think there was a man aboard who had any clothes left except those he was wearing, and in some cases they gave up part of them."

Captain Diehl had high praise for a *Morro Castle* stewardess named Lena Schwartz: "Forgetting the ordeal she'd been through herself, Miss Schwartz turned to with a will, ministering to her fellow passengers who were worse off. You can say for me that she was a mighty fine woman."

As soon as the surfboat was unloaded, the coastguardmen went back to where their Pickett boat and a lifeboat were last seen. "The lifeboat was gone," Moulton said, "and the Pickett boat was there rolling helplessly, about to capsize. We ran down by them and hollered to know what the trouble was. They said their engine had stopped and they had gotten a fishing boat (the *Paramount*) to take the lifeboat with them. Even if we had had the power to take the Pickett in tow, we could not have done it, as our gas was getting low. We decided the only thing to do was for me to board the Pickett and see if I could get her engines running. The regular engineer was not on board, he having gone on liberty before the fire started.

"I got aboard her some way, and straightened up to take a look. I saw a dead woman laying across the stern, dead lying on top of the cabin; the portside of the deck and cabin were red, dripping blood. In the after-cabin were the most forelorn men and women I have ever seen, and all with hardly a rag on. Bilge matter was on the after-cabin floor and in the engine room forward, and everywhere one of the worst smells I have ever smelt where they had vomited. A fish factory is cologne compared to the smell on that boat.

"One of the boys was on the stern in his underwear, trying to get the rest of his clothes on. I did not know the reason at the time, but have since heard from the crew that he deserves a lot of credit, which he is not getting. When the engine stopped on them, they were trying to come up to three women with life preservers on; he went overboard and managed to pull them close enough for the rest to get them on board. His name is Monroe Wilson of Marshalburg, North Carolina.

"I managed to get the engine running. . . . We ran around after that for a while, but could find nothing but dead with life preservers on. We picked up a few of them, but it was such a job to get them on board and they would soon be on the beach anyway. The fellow in charge thought it best to get those in cabins to a doctor, and leave those already dead alone. . . .

"How many we pulled out of the water, I don't know. I kept count up to fifty-six; the Skipper says one hundred and sixteen in all."

The *Morro Castle*'s number one lifeboat, carrying Chief Engineer Eban S. Abbott, was now nearing the beach. The seas kept swiping them and sending little shudders down the boat's spine, until finally they got her at a right angle with the surf. Then only the man at the tiller worked; the others held on to thwarts or oarlocks and kept shooting glances seaward, toward the one good wave, as yet unseen, that would carry them all the way inshore. They looked anxious and afraid, as though the proximity of land and the sudden traffic of smaller craft had made them want to put the sea forever behind them.

"Some of them were seasick," Milton Stevenson,

a waiter, in the boat, said. "A couple were yellow around the gills. The nervous strain and excitement had gotten the boys, I think, and they were jittery, because I remember I said to Nemoresky, a waiter, whom I'd played cards with, 'How about a game of pinochle?' Because he looked so yellow it amazed me at the time."

Abbott's white full-dress uniform, in a boat heading for shore with only three passengers, was now a liability, and as Dr. Cochrane, one of the three passengers, put it afterward: "I turned to look at the shore and saw Abbott taking his insignia off his shoulders. I heard him say—we were within sight of the *Morro Castle* at the time—'I will be jailed for this.'"

It was Abbott who first showed interest in the number of passengers in the boat and who personally went to the trouble of taking a count. When he came up with 29 crewmen, 3 passengers, he said, "If we go ashore with only three passengers, we'll be arrested."

Fred Walther, the ordinary seaman sitting next to Abbott, said that Abbott "kept saying that we should not go ashore, that it was too dark and the shore was too rocky around here."

"Row away from here," he kept saying, according to Dr. Cochrane. "We better get in a lane with the ships."

Fred Walther drew this picture of the boat's actual grounding the next morning: "When the boat grounded

on shore, people got out on all sides. They all wanted
to feel the ground beneath them, but it was sand one
minute and water the next."

Abbott was no sooner on the beach than he started
telling the seamen not to talk to reporters. "He walked
unaided," Walther said. "I went in the same car to the
police station with him. He wanted to know if another
boat came in. Fellow says 'yes' and Abbott says, 'How
many passengers?' Fellow says, 'None.' Abbott says, 'At
least we have three.'

"He was in his uniform, with his hat on. After we
went to the second police station he took the insignia
'Chief Engineer' off his hat, and after that he changed
his clothes completely."

"Abbott seemed to be all right as soon as he got to
shore," Quartermaster Fleischman, the man in charge of
the boat, said. "He walked over to the beach. Nobody
assisted him."

Dr. Cochrane, meanwhile, having walked to the
boardwalk in his bathrobe (or overcoat, it never became
clear), was taken in a model-A Ford by some local
people to, of all places, the Spring Lake Bathing Pavil-
ion.

The whole world knew of the disaster now. Planes
were flying to the scene, Coast Guard cutters racing to

it under full steam. Setting-up exercises, organ reveilles and chats to housewives were being interrupted by dramatic news bulletins.

The NBC setting-up-exercise instructor, for example, was just finishing his final Saturday-morning calisthenics when he noticed a sudden tension behind the glass of the control booth. After signing off he went into the booth, heard the bulletin about the *Morro Castle* and, paling, sank in a chair. Only a few weeks before he had obtained an a.b. job on the ship for his son, Arthur Bagley, Jr., the young man who had seen passengers throwing lighted cigarettes into a wastepaper basket. Bagley senior had to wait hours before learning that his son was among those saved.

Meanwhile, crowds of friends and relatives were beginning to gather at the Ward Line pier at the foot of Wall Street in New York City where the liner was to have docked. Several came innocently, not yet knowing what had happened, while others, already informed, came under the delusion that their loved ones were still somehow going to disembark where the Ward Line tickets said they would. Still others argued that the three rescue ships would go to their own respective docks in Brooklyn, Manhattan and Staten Island.

"The *Luckenback* docks are in Brooklyn," they said. "The Furness Line docks are in the fifties. Why wait here? The *Morro Castle*'s anchored out there some-where and no one's on it anyway."

In the end, despite the appearance of ambulances from St. Vincent's, Knickerbocker, Bellevue, Flower, Re-ception and Marine Hospitals, and the obviously elabo-rate pains of the police for the arrival of the rescue ships, the question of where to wait became such an agonizing one that hundreds of relatives and friends began gravitating toward the New Jersey shore itself. They took trains, cars and taxis to Sea Girt, Brielle, Spring Lake and Asbury Park, and mingled there with thousands of vacationers in raincoats who lined the beaches and boardwalks to watch lifeguards rush into the water as survivors appeared on sandbars, jetties and debris.

Forty survivors were being treated at Spring Lake alone, where the supply of oxygen was running so low that Captain Charles Brand, in charge of the first-aid station at the beach, sent out the urgent call for more oxygen to every hospital in the vicinity.

At Brielle, coastguardmen with pulmotors were try-ing to revive a number of those brought to the beach. One thirteen-year-old boy, given up for dead, began to move his fingers slightly after a pulmotor had been applied. A heavy rain followed this miraculous return to life, forcing the guardmen to transfer him, in rhythm with the pulmotor, to a small shack just off the beach. Men ran to lunch stands and homes for kettles of hot water in an effort to warm the boy's slender, sunburned body. He had dark hair and thick black lashes that flickered and wavered between life and death.

Suddenly a doctor came in, bent over the boy and motioned to a nurse to hand him a needle and syringe. The doctor made the injection and after a long anxious moment the boy's eyelashes began to move more rapidly. The doctor looked up, nodding his head. The boy would live.

Captain Ziezler of the fishing boat *Diane* had had ten bodies pointed out to him by Governor Moore's plane. Three children were among those picked up, two boys and a girl. "One of the little boys had dressed in a hurry or in the dark," Captain Ziezler said. "His right shoe was on his left foot, and his pajamas were upside down. An old woman wore one shoe and a corset. She had on no life preserver, and this was true of others who had drowned.

"What made us come back in was that one of the men was still alive, and we figured he had a chance. We worked on him all the way in, but he died."

Meanwhile, as troops, buses, ambulances and crews of doctors and nurses began converging on the Jersey shore, relatives went from police station to fire house to Coast Guard shack to private residence and listened eagerly to survivors who might tell them what had happened to the husband, wife or child they could not find. Since the Saturday editions of newspapers were already on the stands when news of the disaster began to accumulate, the radio was the only source of information. From 6:00 A.M. on, the air waves were filled with reports:

There is great confusion over the dead and living because of the many different beaches where survivors are appearing out of the surf. . . . A fog settling over the coast line is making the rescue work harder. . . . Four survivors at Spring Lake show symptoms of pneumonia; Helen Brodie among them has a temperature of 104°. . . . There are already bodies in the Mannesquan Morgue, at the Coast Guard Station in Sea Girt, at the Point Pleasant First Aid Station, all waiting to be identified. . . . John L. Moran, one of the steamboat inspectors who passed the *Morro Castle* last May is stunned: "It's like having the Empire State Building burn. . . ." The ship [on its way to Havana] is said to have carried ammunition listed in the manifest as "sporting goods," but the Ward Line does not know to which political faction in Cuba it was going. When the fire broke out, however, the 750 tons of cargo were mostly noninflammable fruit. . . . Rumors of sabotage, resulting from labor troubles, are to be investigated. . . . Captain Wilmott made a fatal decision before he died. The *Castle* was so far ahead of schedule that her speed was reduced at 10:30 Friday forenoon to such an extent that one of her six boilers was allowed to cool. Otherwise, the ship might have been in Quarantine by the time the fire was discovered. . . . An outstanding swimming feat was that of Antonio Mata, twenty, a Cuban messboy, who swam from ship to shore without a lifebelt and was rescued from the surf just as he collapsed. . . . Passengers are to be taken to the Hotel New Yorker, the crew to the Seamen's Institute. . . . First Assistant Engineer Bujia refused to discuss the catastrophe other than to say that the fire seemed to have started in a half dozen places at once and to hazard the suspicion that it had been "set." . . . Members of crew, who were talkative when first picked up, grew silent and refused to comment when officers told them to shut up. . . . A relief train will be leaving Spring Lake sometime after noon [Saturday], with the survivors in care of five nurses from the Monmouth County Volunteer Red Cross. . . . John H. Andrews and his son John T. of New Canaan had canceled their trip on the *Morro Castle* because, on the morning they were to sail, the moving men reminded them that they were supposed to move that day. . . .

19

It was near 8:00 A.M. and several ships were leaving the vicinity of the *Morro Castle*. The *Monarch of Bermuda* had 71 survivors aboard, the *City of Savannah* 65, the *Andrea S. Luckenback* 26, and the *President Cleveland* none.

The burning ship looked very tender. She was listing to starboard from the small lake which had formed below and sending off great billows of smoke low over the water behind her. Her steel from the water line upward was cherry red beneath its charred exterior; she was perhaps hotter along her entire length than at any time since the fire started. And yet for those on the departing ships, the separation in space from the heat seemed to lag behind the separation in time. The fire was already remote; it had been experienced but could no longer be imagined.

Survivors especially noticed this botched, discarded look of the *Morro Castle* as they were drawn away to safety. It was as if they were seeing from a plane a city that they knew well. They could pinpoint little smoking things here and there where they had dined or danced or pushed a puck along a shuffleboard, but from this distance it was all one, the burning helpless hulk lay impaled upon the water, a huge maritime disgrace.

A man who saw the ship from a plane, Carl Sparling, a staff reporter for the *New York World-Telegram,* had a similar reaction. His chartered plane hovered over the burning hulk as a moth might have, and Sparling's at once intimate and remote account encompasses perfectly the reactions of the survivors as the rescue ships departed.

"A white rolling plume of smoke billowed for miles behind the ship, as far as the eye could see over the gray and angry water. Despite the flame that filled the depths, the ship seemed from the air to be burning almost lazily. There was a listlessness in the way the smoke arose in the heavy atmosphere and went off in the wind close against the breaking waves. The heat had seared the paint from her sides. Nothing was left of the super-structure except the black steel skeleton.

"Grotesquely, the ship rode at anchor, her iron safely in the water and the green shore within sight.

"Occasionally as the flames found some new vital spot in the depths the smoke billowed up with fresh intensity and assumed tinges of dirty yellow and green. No flames were visible except from almost directly above. The heat came in through our windows in acrid blasts as the plane swooped down and near.

"The men huddled in the bow were oblivious to what was happening in the air. They did not look up. They did not move. Over the scene there was an air of detachment, of inertia, as if life had come to a still, poised despair there under a black heaven that had come down to sit heavy upon a foaming gray sea."

While Carl Sparling was watching from his vantage point in the air, a New York pilot boat (a small tug) came in from the north, reared off the *Morro Castle's* bow and put a small powerboat over. On the bow Warms and his men, burned, coughing and ready to collapse, watched and waited. They did not know it yet, but the most gruelling part of the whole disaster was ahead.

When the power boat reached the *Morro Castle's* bow, a man named Swenson, a New York Harbor Pilot, called up to Warms, "You want to be taken off?"

"No," Warms said.

"You want a tow? We'll tow you and it won't cost you a thing."

"Can you tow us?"

"What kind of line you got?"

"Eight-inch."

The offer of a small tug to tow a 12,000-ton liner through that sea struck more than one man on the bow of the *Morro Castle* as ridiculous, but Warms, so worn by now that his face looked like hammered tin, turned to his men and said, "You heard that, fellows, he said it won't cost us anything for a tow. You know, after they land us in harbor these fellows forget things like that."

Warms, as a captain with an uncertain future and under the pressure of the salvage law, was reluctant to turn his ship over. He doubted his own judgment and had even asked Captain Diehl of the *City of Savannah* to radio the ship's owners for instructions as to "what he should do," another example of the debilitating effect of the radio on captains at sea. A man who had had his rightful authority as chief officer undermined would naturally, as temporary captain of the same ship, want to be told what to do. A great deal was made of this remark of Warms ("You heard him, fellows") during the various investigations that followed. Critics said that it showed a disproportionate concern for saving the company money, and that the sending of the S O S might have been delayed for the same reason.

But after the staggering experience he had been through, and having failed to obtain instructions from New York before the *City of Savannah's* departure from the scene, Warms's willingness to accept a tow from so small a boat, so long as the tow was free, is at least understandable. He was still, if now only instinctively, trying to be loyal to his company.

At any rate the deal never carried through, for while they were talking the Coast Guard Cutter *Tampa,* 240 feet long, weighing 1,800 tons and with a 100-man crew under Lt. Commander Earl G. Rose, rounded up in the wind and came out on the *Morro Castle's* portside. The cutter, the only Coast Guard boat capable of towing a ship as large as the *Castle,* had made the run traveling at 16 knots from her Staten Island base in two hours.

Warms shouted down to Swenson, "Will you go over and ask him what he is going to do?"

Swenson waved, "All right," and when he came back he said, "They're going to put a twelve-inch hawser aboard you and tow you to New York. Commander Rose thinks you ought to get your ship up north and attempt to salvage it with the aid of the New York fire-boats."

Warms said, "Can you go aft and put a line on the quarter to help steer us? The helm is hard over."

"All right, and it won't cost you anything."

The Cutter *Tampa* had meanwhile gone ahead, or seaward, of the *Morro Castle* and anchored about 260 yards away. A surfboat was lowered with a Coast Guard officer standing in the stern sheets, a coxswain, and eight coastguardmen at oars. The crew aboard the cutter then passed a four-inch running line, or leader line, into the surfboat and the boat rode it down to the bow of the *Morro Castle*.

"Have you any power on your winch?" the Coast Guard officer, his legs and hips swaying in unison with the play of the boat, shouted up through a megaphone to Warms.

"No!"

"Well, throw a heaving line and take this leader line. Haul it aboard and we will bend it on the hawser."

It is difficult for a layman unfamiliar with the sea to appreciate what these men were to attempt. The *Morro Castle* was absolutely powerless, her winches were useless. Any line from the *Tampa,* therefore, had to be brought to the deck of the *Morro Castle* by man power alone. And since the men aboard the *Tampa* could merely pay out the hawser from their end, all the work, the pulling, had to be done by the men aboard the

Castle who were already so exhausted they could barely stand.

The men rowing the surfboat, meanwhile, had themselves become so exhausted in their efforts to hug the *Castle's* bow that they finally began to give way to the heavy seas pushing them aft along the skin of the ship. Warms tried several times to get the heaving line to them, but since he could only go as far aft as the flaming superstructure, and the eight trained oarsmen were no more able to stay near the ship than the *Morro Castle's* boat crews had been earlier, his efforts failed.

Lt. Commander Rose saw through binoculars that his oarsmen were wearing themselves out and immediately communicated with Swenson, whose powerboat finally took over the four-inch leader line and succeeded in getting it to the *Castle's* bow.

After Warms had made fast his end of the 4-inch leader line, which was tied to the 12-inch hawser on the *Tampa's* deck, it took the concerted effort of every man on the *Castle's* bow, fourteen men, just to raise the 4-inch leader line out of the water.

Now the men on the *Tampa* could pay out as much of the 12-inch hawser as they wanted, but they knew that the more of it they did pay out, the more the tide and current would add to its weight. It was up to Warms and his men to haul in the 4-inch leader line, over 200 fathoms of it, and then see, when they came to the end of it, if they could lift the 12-inch hawser out of the sea. They would, therefore, be most exhausted at the very moment when the hawser, stretched through 260 yards of sea, would most resemble a gigantic boa constrictor.

The powerboat tried to help by dragging a bight of the hawser through the water while the men on the bow pulled from their end on the 4-inch leader line, but in the end it was up to the men on the *Morro Castle*'s bow to get the hawser aboard. It took two full hours of constant pulling, with the sweat running off them and sizzling on the hot deck, to raise the hawser out of the water.

Inch by inch, with a cadence that made them wince in unison and curse, they got about fifty fathoms aboard, made it fast on four bitts, took a few turns around the mast and put two half hitches in it. With the job done, and panting from the exertion, they fell where they stood, often on top of one another.

"Hackney, signal——" Warms started to say, and stopped to pull some air into his lungs. The experience of the last eight hours had made cereal of his body's fiber; he felt weak and dreamy and could barely tense his muscles. But something, perhaps the enormous insolence of what had happened to him since Wilmott's death, coupled with the wildly insistent idea that the ship was still a ship under his command, made poi-

sonous energy of his bile. "Tell them by semaphore that
the towline is made fast."

The reply—"slip the anchor chain"—was uninten-
tionally ironic, for Warms could neither raise the anchor
chain nor "slip" it into the sea. It had to be cut, and
with the only tool available, a little hacksaw from the
carpenter shop beneath the forecastle head.

Whether Warms refused to ask Commander Rose for
more appropriate steel-cutting equipment from the
Tampa, or Commander Rose, ignorant of what equipment Warms had aboard, did not think it proper to in-
terfere, was never made clear. But while much superior equipment lay unused aboard the *Tampa,* Warms
and his men, taking turns on a hacksaw used for cutting
lead pipe, BX cable and the like, spent three more hours
cutting through a forged steel link.

The wind on the Beaufort scale, meanwhile, was increasing all the time. It had been at "5" at the time of
the *Tampa*'s arrival, or 26 statute miles an hour, and was
now already at "6," or 34 statute miles an hour.

Had a boatload of coastguardmen with tools and
equipment boarded the *Morro Castle* immediately at
8:00 A.M., not only would the hawser have been hauled
aboard faster, but the anchor chain would have been cut
in a matter of minutes. This five-hour loss in time was
to make the difference between salvage and ruin for the
Morro Castle.

Once the chain was severed and the ship freed of the ocean floor, the men on the bow of the *Castle* were to abandon the ship to the *Tampa*. The powerful cutter was then to tow the burning hulk to New York with the pilot boat acting as jury rudder. This meant that the *Morro Castle* crew's only chance of getting off would be just as the chain was severed. Lt. Commander Rose of the *Tampa* had already radioed for a specially constructed Coast Guard lifeboat, a very efficient seagoing, rough-water craft with a turtle-backed bow and stern and a protected midship section. When it arrived, already half loaded with dead bodies hauled from the water on the way out, the men on the *Castle*'s bow, between turns on the hacksaw, began lowering a few belongings.

Rogers, who had gone to the fo'c'sle "to replace the pair of shoes he'd kicked into the water to save the woman," had seen a canary in a cage over one of the seamen's bunks. He had decided then, he said later during vaudeville appearances at the Rialto Theatre, to try to save the bird, and when he went down for it now to lower it into the boat, he noticed a marked change in the fo'c'sle. The place was a compost of odors now, as though its original locker-room smell had multiplied itself, expanded. The air hung in compartments, one hotter than another; there was no flurry or waver other than that of heat itself. He felt inundated by dryness and

heat and, "investigating, noticed that the bulkhead separating the fo'c'sle from number one hold was glowing
a bright red and bellying forward from expansion." The
whole place was about to burst into flame; he had better
alert Captain Warms.

A few minutes before, on deck, while Warms and his
men were laboring with the tiny hacksaw, Rogers had
said, "It's a damn shame that we have to use these five-
and-ten-cent methods." The irony is that he was right;
it *was* a shame, with the *Tampa* so close by. Now here
he was (he said from the stage of the Rialto Theatre),
going down to the fo'c'sle "to save the canary" he'd
seen while searching for a pair of shoes to replace the
ones he'd kicked off in order "to save the woman," only
to discover another real and present danger.

In their definitive book, *Pathological Firesetting,*
Nolan D. C. Lewis and Helen Yarnell write of the
"hero" firesetter: "Throughout they are in and out and
around the scene of the crime, abetting the mass excitement and fear, playing detective, giving advice, assist-
ing firemen, and as a climax become chief witnesses
about whom the trial and newspaper stories center."

Rogers ran up and told Warms, who immediately sent
everybody below, ordering them to bring up every mattress and piece of furniture, anything at all that might
feed a fire, and heave it overboard. The anchor chain
was hanging by a thread, but he figured that if the fire

got forward into the fo'c'sle, the line connecting the ship to the *Tampa* would be set afire. A hawser, whether made of hemp, sisal or jute, could burn.

The *Tampa* had meanwhile taken a strain on the hawser and the giant limb of a line had crunched out of the water and begun to bleed with briny tension. Warms, who had put a buoy line on the anchor chain, finished severing the chain and slipped it free into the sea.

"I will stay here," he called down to the Coast Guard officer in the boat.

"No, it is the commander's orders that you get off the ship."

Now that the ship was free except for her towline to the *Tampa,* the men at once started down ropes into the specially constructed lifeboat. Rogers started down the Jacob's ladder hanging just aft of the bow on the port side, but he suddenly became sick. One minute the lifeboat was in a trough, the next on a crest of sea, with the ladder seemingly hooked to the sky. Rogers tried to study its bobbing movements but the dead people in the boat kept distracting him. "Come on," the men in the boat called, "we'll catch you. Let go!"

He finally dropped in among the dead bodies, and fainted. He became delirious before he reached the *Tampa* and was later, he said, "ordered by the Coast

Guard doctor" to be taken to the Marine Hospital on a stretcher.

Then Warms slid down, the last man off. The knuckles in his right hand had been broken during an attempt to recover Wilmott's body, and his shoulders, elbows, knees and face had been burned. But it wasn't until he landed in the lifeboat, until he relinquished his command, that he noticed these almost comforting little injuries. He had been master of a ship for the shortest time on record.

On the *Tampa,* thick white blankets stamped USCG were brought up from below, and soon guardmen and seamen alike, the one dry and wearing dungarees and zippered jackets, the other wet, shivering and wrapped in blankets, were sipping hot coffee from the Coast Guard's thick handleless mugs. They warmed their hands against the pock-marked porcelain and let the beany fragrance pass up through their nostrils, the seamen all the while looking with a tired, secret love at the ship they had in tow. . . . She had moved with the wind to where a break in the sky had created a rotunda of light. They could see the steam as the seas reached above her water line.

It was after one thirty when the three vessels, the *Tampa* first, the unmanned *Morro Castle* second, and the pilot boat acting as jury rudder third, started from Sea Girt to New York.

For four hours they swayed and slipped through increasingly heavy seas while the wind on the Beaufort Scale indicated a force of almost forty miles an hour. They passed Spring Lake, Belmar, the Shark River Inlet, Bradley Beach, Ocean Grove, and then came abeam of Asbury Park where, through the rain, they could see the outline of streets, the powdery pastels of stucco buildings and the almost imperceptible, minute-hand movement of vehicles. Progress became so slow that it was almost as if the vast and curving shelf of water were itself turning and bringing New York closer.

At this point, while plowing just north of Asbury Park, the wind on the hulk's starboard bow turned her shoreward, forcing the *Tampa* to steam offshore, the pilot boat inshore, in an effort to get the hulk back on her northward course. The stern was red-hot, however, and when the wind, as the hulk turned, caught and fed this heat, the stern line burned and parted, leaving the *Tampa* to tow the *Morro Castle* without a jury rudder.

Lt. Commander Rose said later, "It is next to impossible to tow a ship without power in a rough sea unless she has another boat steering her with a line astern."

However, the northeaster had been increasing in force from the time of the *Tampa*'s arrival, and if there had been no delay with the hawser and anchor chain, if the procession from Sea Girt had started, say, about 10:00 A.M. instead of 1:30 P.M., the wind would not have been as strong as it was when the ships came abeam of Asbury, nor would the fire at the stern of the *Morro Castle* have progressed to the point where it was capable of burning the line. The stricken ship might have been well up Sandy Hook and in the hands of the New York fireboats before the storm reached the point where it was able to take charge.

"We got to the point where we were making no headway," Lt. Commander Rose said, "and we were nearly abeam of her trying to get her out to sea. Soundings showed that we were approaching shore."

The *Tampa* had to increase her revolutions until the 12-inch hawser seemed to shrink in circumference from the strain. Not a drop of sea was left in that crunching line; it was straight and stiff as a girder. Finally and suddenly it broke with such force that a shackle at the *Castle's* end of the towing line snapped back and struck the *Tampa's* propeller, fouling it. For a few seconds the plight of the *Morro Castle* was forgotten, for with the torn and shredded hawser entangled about the *Tampa's* propeller, the strain on the propeller shaft forced the thrust bearing out of true. There was the immediate and grave danger of the cutter's drifting against the still burning hulk and herself being set ablaze.

"Let go the anchor!" bellowed Lt. Commander Rose to his men.

They did and the cutter was held fast; the sea began to widen between the cutter and the burning ship.

It was only then that the *Morro Castle* came back into the realm of reality, came back with such force that several men aboard the *Tampa* could not restrain their tears. The sky had darkened and the sea looked higher now and more metallic, like a huge and menacing junk yard except that the topmost scraps kept flying shoreward and banging against the side of the *Morro Castle*. The whole black weight of the place kept shifting and turning as from tremors underneath, which made its power on the surface look that much more gratuitous and awful. It was this brutal heedlessness and mangling of the sea around the stricken ship that made her look so helpless and pathetic.

Two lifeboats still locked on their chocks came into view as she veered round with the wind; boat falls and ropes dragged limply through the water; the whole gutted superstructure looked like an unfair exposure of the ship designer's dream.

There was a terrible poignancy in the sight of her as she swayed and creaked like a huge uprooted buoy and started sliding southwest with the wind and racing sea. No elemental necessity had figured in her downfall, no great storm, no battle, not even a collision—nothing but incompetence, negligence and the irresistible impulse of an unbalanced man.

It was as if sanity itself were drifting away with her.

20

If Billy Rose, whose spectacular "Jumbo" was then in rehearsal for its opening at the Hippodrome in New York, had been asked where the beaching of the *Morro Castle* would get the best theatrical results, he could not have chosen a better location than Asbury Park, New Jersey.

With a precision that five tugboats could not have improved upon, the ship came to rest broadside with the boardwalk at the foot of Sunset Avenue between a long jetty and Convention Hall, the three-million-dollar steel pier the City of Asbury Park had built the year before.

Guests at the Berkeley-Carteret and Monterey hotels could see the stricken liner from their windows. Restaurants, cocktail lounges, chance machines, shooting galleries, kiddy rides, frozen-custard and hot-dog stands formed a kind of family circle around the charred salamander of a ship.

In Convention Hall itself, where ex-champ Primo Carnera was training for a tour of South America, radio station WCAP, on the northern promenade of the building, had a ringside seat. Tom Burley, the announcer, in addition to having the stern of the ship almost in his lap, could see the crowds forming to his left, hear the fire engines coming, and watch the concessionaires rip down their boards and turn on their lights for what was to become an unheard-of boom in business for September.

No unrehearsed and unpredictable happening in American history has ever received such immediate first-hand reporting as this virtual mooring of a ship in the studio of a radio station itself. If Tom Burley had reached his listeners a second sooner with the news, he would have been predicting rather than reporting events.

Still much too hot to board when she arrived at 7:35 on Saturday night, the towering hulk was stared at in wonder by thousands who crowded round her on the beach, in much the same way the Lilliputians stared at Gulliver. Before it grew dark and the authorities arrived, young men swam out to feel her, and brought back flaps of paint that had hung loosely from her side. These young men immediately became experts and expounded theories, while others on the beach studied the scroll-like flaps. No one argued. The nearness of the ship, the red showing through her parts, and the try-pots that had once been lifeboats, made everyone strangely quiet and agreeable. The anxiety of death belonged to their existence too, and in that sense the ship had a secret hold on them.

"Look at that!" someone shouted as a great breaker, hitting the weather side of the ship, sent spray over her stacks. "Do you suppose they're throwing water on it from the other side?"

The first man aboard the ship the next morning was James Kontajones, the city engineer of Asbury Park, who had spent three years on the *Morro Castle* prior to his present job. He went out in a rowboat, grabbed the rope to which Phelps, Jr., had clung for several hours, and went up hand over hand. Coastguardmen then shot him a line from a Lyle gun and proceeded to rig up a breeches buoy between the stern of the ship and the ground floor of Convention Hall.

A fierce argument started between an Asbury Park official and a representative of one of the underwriters, who had rushed to the scene, claiming that he had authority over the ship, that the city official's authority ended where the beach ended. He was going to be the first to cross over in the breeches buoy, he said; not only that, he was not going to allow the official to cross over at all. In that case, the official said, the underwriter would have to swim, or rather, fly, out to the ship, since Asbury Park had authority over both the beach and Convention Hall.

Bitter words followed, while the waves slapped against the steel piles beneath the pier and the breeches buoy hung limp and unused over the water. When the underwriters' representative was threatened with arrest by Asbury Park police, he showed his credentials to Chief Boatswain's Mate William J. Butler of the Coast Guard, who decided that the underwriters' representative had authority.

Meanwhile thousands of housewives along the boardwalk were fascinated by the breeches buoy, which resembled a giant clothesline. When the underwriter finally climbed in and was pulled over, above the surf, to the stern of the ship, they cheered, prompting the man to wave with all the aplomb of a daredevil walking a wire over the gorge at Niagara.

Only two men boarded the ship before the underwriter—James Kontajones, the city engineer, and Robert W. Hodge of the Coast Guard. Both were farther forward when the underwriter boarded, but Hodge could see him picking up the purses women had left on deck before abandoning ship.

Relatives and friends were still going from cot to cot in a desperate identification tour at the improvised morgue at Camp More; four railroad baggage cars at Sea Girt were still to be loaded with the dead; the remains of bodies on the ship itself (mostly bones) had not been put in pillow cases yet, and the underwriters' representative was picking up ladies' handbags!

Later, when reporters crossed on the breeches buoy, the representative charged them five dollars for the right to board the ship. "For liquor for the firemen," he said. When the newsmen paid without an argument, he added, "You can't go far without a gas mask, either, and the use of one will cost you five dollars more." One reporter who asked about a flashlight, was given one temporarily for a dollar.

"What gets me," cried a city official, "is that the gas masks belong to Asbury Park!"

A kind of ghoulish competition followed. The representative charged ten dollars for boarding the ship, while, above Convention Hall, a huge garish sign went up:

Twenty-five cents to see the
SS Morro Castle
Benefit of the families of the dead.

Meanwhile, thousands of automobiles rolled into Asbury Park and the "parking lot" was born. Home owners rented rooms, lawns, garages, set up lemonade stands, and talk reached fever pitch around Convention Hall over making the burning hulk a permanent museum piece at Asbury Park.

"You don't have to buy or rent that ship," the mayor was told. "There she is in your own front yard. Raise a city flag on her and stake your claim."

Someone suggested hopefully that if the claim went through, a gangplank or catwalk could be built from the Hall to the ship. There was talk about laying planking across the deck beams as soon as they were cool enough. Admission could be charged. Uniformed guides could lead groups about as they did at the Empire State Building in New York.

It was the underwriter's day, however, once his authority was accepted and the breeches buoy became his own private toll bridge. He sent ashore for sandwiches and beer, reluctant to leave the ship even for a minute.

One man who boarded the ship, saying he was a reporter, came on a mission never made public. He paid the ten-dollar fee without protest, put on a gas mask, and immediately started forward along the twisted sagging deck on the starboard side where firemen with wet steaming clothes were fastening a hose to the rail to keep it off the hot deck.

He paid very little attention to the firemen, however, or to anyone else. He had his own flashlight and knew where he was going and how to get there. He kept leaping from one steel deck beam to another, past freakishly untouched patches of planking on which rested high-heeled shoes, vanity cases and men's hats; past twisted elevator shafts, bent mail chutes and deck scuppers clogged with lead from electric cables that had melted and then hardened again; past distorted doorframes, corrugated bulkheads and dining rooms where every bit of wood was gone. In some sections the masses of smoke and gas would have been impassable without a mask, in others the man's rubber heels stuck to the hot steel.

When he reached stateroom number three, where Catherine Cochrane died while O'Sullivan was looking for her in stateroom number five, he stuck his flashlight through a port from which the glass had melted and saw what looked like the remains of a bombing. Fine gray dust powdered everything. Form and outline took on all the precarious beauty of something filigreed and very old. There was something both accelerated and archaeological about the place; everything was still so hot and yet so hopelessly finished.

The man went in anyway, through the rugless gassy corridor and into the doorless cabin itself. He found the bedsteads melted, the mattress gone, and the remains of a body crumpled in the bedsprings. Whoever this man was, he knew that Catherine Cochrane had had her diamonds with her and not in the purser's safe. He took out a key and, with the searchlight in his left hand, the key in the right, began carefully sifting through the crumpled bones for the diamonds he knew were there.

The masked face of this man, the key going through the springs like a strong probing fingernail, and the intent posture of his back, as though bending low over someone, indicated far more than curiosity over the fire. He was well dressed, his tie had obviously been chosen and knotted with care, and he was no doubt going to discard his burned shoes the moment he got home. He was a man no one watching could have known—a pragmatist whose only guide was his knowledge of the diamonds. He got what he came for—and left.

The next day the underwriters' representative disappeared and was being sought by the police for questioning about what the Ward Line called "a large amount of unaccounted for personal property."

He was later brought before the Monmouth County grand jury, but the Assistant Attorney General refused to discuss the findings and the case gradually died. The personal belongings of several seamen were found in the crew's quarters, among them a bag owned by Assistant Electrician Percy Miller in which were a dozen mission tracts and a Bible. . . . In the office of the assistant purser on D deck, a strongbox was found to contain an eighth of an inch of reddish dust, the remains of currency. . . . In the liner's safe, a box one foot long, three inches wide and six inches deep had protected and kept intact the valuable jewels of Renee Mendez Capote, daughter of General Domingo Mendez Capote, former Vice President of Cuba and head of the 1931 Anti-Machado Revolutionary Junta in New York. . . . On deck a medal belonging to Chief Electrician William Justis was found. The medal had been awarded to Justis in 1926 for heroism at sea, when as a member of the crew of the *President Roosevelt* he had helped rescue the crew of the *Antinoe* in mid-Atlantic.

On the second day, Captain William A. Hall boarded the ship to represent the Ward Line and to search for Wilmott's remains, which the district attorney's office wanted for analysis.

Captain Hall knew the *Morro Castle* intimately and made the search in the presence of Carl Bischoff, the Mayor of Asbury Park. There was no doubt in Hall's mind as to which cabin Captain Wilmott had occupied, and in view of the fact that both Quartermaster Fleischman and Acting Captain Warms had failed in their attempts to remove Wilmott's body during the fire, the result of this search remains intriguing today.

"We went into Captain Wilmott's quarters," Carl Bischoff said. "We made a careful search, but found no trace of bones or charred remains, and no evidence that the captain was cremated following his death. In our tour of the upper decks, we came upon no additional bodies."

The next day, however, Fire Chief William S. Taggart found the remains of a body on the same cabin floor. Did someone put the remains there *after* Hall and Bischoff had made their search, or did Hall and Bischoff make such a superficial search that they did not recognize a man's skull when they saw one?

"The first clue I had to the location of Wilmott's body," Taggart said, "was a bunch of keys which I found near what must have been the doorway leading from his quarters to the bridge. The keys bore a tag which was labeled 'Captain.'

"When I entered the cabin, I found that the metal legs of the bed had melted. The body must have slid forward. It wasn't really his face, though. It was just a skull. Then I found the bones of what must have been his legs and arms.

"I was convinced the cabin was Wilmott's because in one corner the safe stood, and on top of that a radio."

Captain Hall claimed that he knew the ship better than Fire Chief Taggart did and that, when he entered the captain's cabin the day before, it was empty.

The body found by Taggart nevertheless became known as Wilmott's body and was taken in what looked like a plumber's tool case to New York for analysis.

Doctor Alexander Gettler, City Toxicologist, said, "Since volatile poisons burn off, only metal poisons could be checked. We found traces of lead, copper, bismuth and barium, but that doesn't mean much. The buttons, metal, pipes, wires, all were melted and may have contaminated the bones."

Since such metal poisons usually require months to cause death to human beings, the autopsy to determine the cause of Captain Wilmott's death—if the body examined was Wilmott's to begin with—was a failure.

During the weeks that followed, while theories as to the cause of the fire became more and more numerous and conflicting, while suits against the Ward Line were filed by virtually every survivor, and investigations by both the Steamboat Inspectors and the District Attorney's office continued, the wet, decomposing cargo in the hold of the ship began to disconcert concessionaires who were thinking in terms of a Christmas tourist rush. They had no objection to the ship's remaining at Asbury but wished she didn't smell so foully. Even Primo Carnera, who had first looked upon the ship as unfair competition, changed his mind when twice as many people as previously paid the 25¢ admission to see him spar in Convention Hall's auditorium. The crowd was the thing, and every businessman as far inland as Steinbach's Department Store realized it. In fact, the influx of motorists throughout October was a contributing factor in making Asbury Park one of the first cities in the United States to install parking meters.

Meanwhile, George Alagna, who had been arrested in New York and brought in handcuffs to Foley Square on suspicion of sabotage, was released for lack of evidence. In the end, it was his Grand Jury testimony against the Ward Line, Captain Warms, Chief Engineer Abbott and all the other "madmen on the bridge" at the time of the fire that helped bring about the handing out of indictments on December 3, 1934.

How many times Warms visited Asbury Park after this indictment is not known. Living, as he was, at Morristown, New Jersey, "on the generosity of the Ward Line," a land-locked sea captain awaiting trial, he must have come often to watch the salvage crew take his ship apart. If he was there on the evening of December twenty-fourth, when a Christmas tree suddenly came into sparkling existence on the bow of the ship where he had spent his last ounce of strength before boarding the *Tampa,* the thought must surely have repeated itself in his mind: Is it real or am I dreaming?

Warms and Abbott were accused of misconduct, negligence and inattention to duty. The charges against Warms were that he failed (1) to divide the sailors in equal watches, (2) to keep himself advised of the extent of the fire, (3) to maneuver, slow down or stop the vessel, (4) to have the passengers aroused, (5) to provide the passengers with life preservers, (6) to take steps for the protection of lives, (7) to organize the crew to fight the fire properly, (8) to send distress signals promptly, (9) to see that the passengers were put in lifeboats and that the lifeboats were lowered, (10) to control and direct the crew in the lifeboats after the lifeboats had been lowered.

The charges against Abbott were that he failed (1) to assign members of his department to proper posts during the fire, (2) to report to his own station in the engine room and consequently gave no instructions to his men. The indictment also charged that although he knew the water pressure to be inadequate, he did nothing to increase it. He also had charge of the ship's lighting and generators, the indictment continued, and did nothing when they failed. He did not report to his lifeboat station (boat 6), ". . . and as a matter of fact made no effort to rescue anyone else after he left the vessel in number 1."

In January, 1936, after many postponements, Warms, though he had been captain of the *Morro Castle* for only eight hours, was sentenced to two years' imprisonment. Abbott was sentenced to four. And for the first time in local maritime history, a court imposed sentence upon an official of a steamship company, Henry E. Cabaud, tall, white-haired, executive vice president of the Line. He was fined five thousand dollars and got a suspended one-year sentence for "willful" negligence. The company was found guilty of the same charge and fined ten thousand dollars, and the judge added that he regretted the penalty was insufficient, according to the statute.

After the verdict Warms said, "It's hard for a jury to understand the conditions which confronted me. Having no knowledge or experience of the way of the sea, the jury probably didn't comprehend what it means to suddenly battle against a racing sea, the worst storm for years along the Alantic Coast, and a fire which was sweeping the vessel. To have done more than I did would have been superhuman.

"Then, again, only in this country are such cases tried by laymen juries. In England and other foreign countries they are heard and tried before admiralty courts."

In April, 1937, the sentences against Warms and Abbott (Cabaud and the company did not appeal) were reversed by the United States Circuit Court of Appeals, which unanimously set aside the conviction with the remark that "Warms had maintained the best traditions of the sea by staying on the vessel until the bridge had burned from under him."

The Court had no commendation for the behavior of Abbott, and he too was found not guilty of willful negligence. "Smoke" caused his shaky behavior, and therefore he was not responsible.

That afternoon Warms was called to a neighbor's telephone in Morristown, New Jersey, where he was free on bail. He ran out of the neighbor's house shouting, "I've won, I've won!"

"How much?" his plump red-haired wife asked, remembering that they had a sweepstakes' ticket.

"No, no," whooped Warms. "I've won in Court; I'm cleared!" Later he said, "It was the judgment of God. I was innocent and God knew it. Now I'm going back to sea. It is the only work I know."

Meanwhile, claims totaling $1,250,000 had been filed against the Ward Line by survivors and relatives of the dead. The company offered the sum of $890,000, to be divided among the claimants. This latter sum was finally accepted.

The ship itself, which cost $5,000,000, was sold to the Union Shipbuilding Company of Baltimore for $33,605. The hulk was towed first to Gravesend Bay in New York and then to Baltimore, where it was scrapped.

POSTSCRIPT

IN PERSON!
RADIO HERO ROOERS
TELLS INSIDE STORY OF
MORRO CASTLE DISASTER*

The one indisputable fact that emerged from the hundreds of thousands of words of testimony taken during the *Morro Castle* investigation was that George W. Rogers remained at his post in the radio room until the S O S message was sent. The American public, shocked by the cowardice and stupidity of other members of the crew, hastened to make Rogers the symbol

* Rialto Theatre Marquee, September, 1934.

of everything fine in the traditions of the sea. He was paraded through his home town of Bayonne, New Jersey, given dinners and presented with awards and gold medals. One enterprising theatrical agent even arranged a vaudeville tour during which Rogers, in a new white uniform purchased by the agent, recounted his *Morro Castle* experiences to RKO audiences for five times what he had earned as a radio operator.

Rogers gave up the sea, and in 1936 joined the police force in Bayonne, New Jersey, where he worked under Lieutenant Vincent Doyle in the radio repair room at police headquarters. The two men spent a great deal of time together, and a recurrent topic of conversation was the unsolved *Morro Castle* fire. Rogers, who had constructed an "electric chair" for the Masons of Hudson County and at meetings would conduct mock electrocutions, told Lieutenant Doyle that he was convinced that the *Morro Castle* fire had been the result of a delayed timing device. He had been quoted repeatedly as saying that the true story of the *Morro Castle* had not been told, and during working hours at the police headquarters he gave Lieutenant Doyle many hints that he knew exactly how and where the fire on the *Morro Castle* started.

"Several times Rogers discussed with me the affinity existent between chemicals," Lieutenant Doyle said. "He was well versed in the chemical action set up between certain acids and compounds that would release huge quantities of oxygen, the gas required to feed a good fire."

Rogers then told Doyle about the incendiary fountain pen that he insisted caused the Black Tom explosion during World War I. He described the pen in detail and said that "experimenting with the thickness of the copper could have guaranteed a delayed action for any period desired."

Doyle, though interested in this Black Tom theory, did not associate it with the unsolved *Morro Castle* fire.

In 1938, however, something happened that brought everything Rogers had said into vivid focus in Lieutenant Doyle's mind. The lieutenant came to work one day and was casually told by Rogers that a package had been delivered for him and was lying on a table in the garage office of headquarters. There was nothing unusual about a package being delivered for the lieutenant; they went together to the garage office and found a note attached to the package:

> *Lieutenant Doyle,*
> *This is a fish-tank heater. Please install the switch in the line cord and see if the unit will work. It should get slightly warm.*

Rogers accompanied Doyle to the radio repair room on the second floor to test the heater. It was all very casual and conversational while Doyle unwrapped the heater, but then when he looked up with the heater plug ready in his hand to insert in the electric light socket, he realized that Rogers had left and that for at least a minute he had been talking to himself. He shrugged, inserted the heater plug, and was immediately knocked off his feet by an explosion and blasted by shrapnel. The fingers of his left hand were blown off, his left thigh was half cut away, and steel scraps cut through his shoes and into his feet. It was clearly an attempt at murder, and for weeks afterward it was a question whether Doyle would live or die. If he had died, Rogers would almost certainly have escaped detection and been given the lieutenant's job.

Doyle lived, however, so that while Rogers was sympathizing with Mrs. Doyle and swearing to Doyle himself, in the hospital, that he was going "to kill the bastard who did this," the police department heads were quietly carrying on an investigation based on Doyle's leads and recollections.

The note attached to the package, they found, had been written on the typewriter in the radio room. A wire in the radio workshop was found to be similar to that used in making the bomb and also corresponded in appearance with a wire on a tube tester used by Rogers. A gray paint found in Rogers's home matched the gray paint with which the bomb had been coated; a cement found in Rogers's home matched the cement with which the bomb had been waterproofed. Finally, a bomb similar to the one sent to Doyle was found under a floor board in Rogers's home.

As the circumstantial evidence accumulated, the story of Rogers and the *Morro Castle* re-emerged. A radio repairman in Bayonne, Preston Dillenbeck, came forward and said, "When Rogers first became a patrolman, he showed me his badge and said he was going to have it chrome-plated. 'Why not have it gold-plated?' I asked jokingly. 'I'll have a gold one soon,' Rogers said, 'because I'm a very ingenious young man.'"

Later he showed Dillenbeck's wife the badge and said, "This one is silver, but someday I expect to have a gold one. There are ways of getting these things."

Preston Dillenbeck would probably never have come forward with this information were it not for the two fraudulent letters that Rogers had had him send to Stanley Ferson, the former Chief Radio Operator of the *Morro Castle*. Dillenbeck had kept the originals of these letters, and when they came to light, Lieutenant Doyle, still in the hospital, said, "When I look at the stumps of my fingers, I wish that he had asked me to quit. He didn't send me any letters, he sent me a bomb."

The Bayonne police quickly communicated with George Alagna, who had attempted suicide in a Queens apartment because of the vicious charges made against him that he had sabotaged the ship. Alagna said that when Rogers joined the ship as a junior operator he told Alagna that he had been assigned to the *Castle* to act as a stool pigeon for the Radiomarine Corporation of America. He was "to obtain information which would result in the dismissal of both Ferson and Alagna." Rogers told Alagna that the letters Ferson received, urging him to resign, had been sent to Ferson by J. B. Duffy, Superintendent of the Radiomarine Corporation of America.

After Rogers's arrest and the many days of questioning that followed, Lieutenant Masterson of the Bayonne Police Department, a much more soft-spoken man than his superior, Captain McGrath, managed to penetrate Rogers's defenses. The police had all the evidence they needed; they had no doubt that Rogers had made and sent the bomb to Doyle. They were just fascinated by this potential murderer in their own department—the hero of a still-unsolved sea disaster.

One day Masterson and Rogers were alone in Mc-Grath's office. The questioning had become desultory and mild; Rogers seemed to be enjoying his cigarette as much as he was McGrath's absence.

"What about that *Morro Castle* fire, George?" Masterson finally put in. "Do you know how it started? Or where? I mean, you were quoted so often as saying that the true story had never been told."

"The fire started in the writing-room locker," Rogers

said. "An incendiary fountain pen started it. The pen had a delayed-action device and it was put in the locker hours before the fire was discovered."

Almost two years had passed since Rogers had described in detail for Doyle the kind of fountain pen that he insisted had caused the Black Tom Explosion during World War I. Could his insistence then, in 1936, when the charges against Warms, Abbott and the Ward Line were being weighed in criminal court, have been an attempt to satisfy a compulsion to divulge the truth about the *Morro Castle* fire? Was he theorizing about the fountain pen, or describing something he had made as accurately as a bomb found under a floor board in his home resembled the bomb that exploded in Doyle's hand?

It was at about this time, while Rogers was confiding in Lieutenant Masterson about what had caused the *Morro Castle* fire, that a stranger visited Lieutenant Doyle in the hospital. This man had been a passenger on the *Morro Castle* during her last ill-fated trip. He had been picked up by a fishing boat after abandoning ship and the next day had been listed in the newspapers as one of the survivors. He had been to Cuba under an assumed name on confidential business having to do with the revolution, however, and for that reason had never testified at any of the investigations that followed the disaster. He wanted no publicity then and he wanted

none in 1938 when he made a special trip to Bayonne
to tell Lieutenant Doyle that on the night before the
Morro Castle fire, Captain Wilmott had told him that
his first act on reaching New York would be to fire
Chief Radio Operator Rogers, that Rogers was a vengeful man capable of acts which might endanger both the
passengers and the ship. He had to be gotten rid of immediately, Wilmott had said, before the ship made another run.

Now when Acting Captain Warms and the other deck
officers first testified before the steamboat inspectors in
New York, they said nothing about Captain Wilmott's
intention to fire Alagna. It was only after Rogers, following his electrifying story of events leading to the sending of the S O S message, offered the information ("reluctantly, because I know it will be misunderstood and
Alagna is my friend") that Wilmott had told him that
he intended to fire Alagna, and after Alagna himself
had followed Rogers to the stand with the fiercest testimony by far against Warms and all the other "madmen
on the bridge," that Warms testified against Alagna.

Rogers, in his efforts to forestall an investigation into
his own past, even blamed Ferson's resignation on
Alagna. When Dickerson Hoover, one of the investigators, asked him, "Did you have any trouble with regard
to radio operators?" Rogers, after a great display of reluctance to testify against "the man who had saved his

life," said, "Now the question you ask entails happenings in the radio department that date back two months before the fatal fire started. There was a strike on board of the radio personnel. Alagna and the third officer . . . went down to the officers' mess and tried to instigate a riot by making up a petition that the food on the *Morro Castle* was very poor, and when the officers and other licensed men down there refused to sign it, Alagna called them a bunch of yellow dogs."

"How do you know that?" Hoover asked.

"Wilmott told me the whole thing just before his death. The trouble culminated in New York when the radio officers called a strike for better living quarters and more wages, waiting for the last minute before the *Morro Castle* sailed before they abandoned the ship. It was held up a couple of hours. It was a mail ship and there was quite a lot of excitement about them holding up the crack Ward Liner. Finally a special agreement with the men on the *Castle* was signed by the company and they went back to work.

"Then, when the third officer got drunk in Havana, he was discharged. . . . The Radiomarine Corporation of America sent me aboard because they expected the other two radio officers would be fired. Mr. Ferson, who was chief operator over me when I took the job, had been with the line three years and had had no trouble until everything blew up when Alagna and the third officer came on. Mr. Ferson quit a while ago and I assumed command as chief operator."

In the next exchange, Rogers went so far as to impute to Alagna a motive for setting fire to the ship.

"What about Captain Wilmott's instructions to get Alagna off the ship?" Hoover asked.

"That was this trip. We hadn't reached New York."

Alagna, by following Rogers on the stand with his incriminating testimony against the Ward Line and the officers on the bridge, unwittingly bolstered Rogers's story. Alagna's unshakable testimony concerning his repeated, futile attempts to get through to Warms for orders to send an S O S finally forced the investigators to recall Warms to the stand. It was only then, after Rogers's testimony about Wilmott's intention to fire Alagna, and after Alagna's own testimony had made it clear that he "could not be bought by the Ward Line," that Warms testified against Alagna.

According to Alagna, the Coast Guard Cutter *Tampa* had not yet reached New York with the *Morro Castle*'s officers and crew when it was boarded from a tug by a representative of the Ward Line, who advised the men to "shut up and you will be taken care of."

When Alagna told him that he intended to tell what he knew, the Ward Line representative, according to Alagna, said, "You had better use some discretion. Nobody will believe you, because you have had strike trouble and a grievance against the Ward Line. Whereas, if you keep quiet, the whole thing will blow over and I will see that you are taken care of."

When Alagna went below and told Rogers what the man had said, Rogers *encouraged* Alagna to testify against the company: "We two must stick together in the name of all those who have perished and we must expose this affair to our utmost ability."

Rogers thereupon turned around and engaged the Ward Line to represent him during the investigation.

"One of the most significant facts in this situation," a spokesman for the American Radio Telegraphists Association said, "is that George W. Rogers is represented by Ward Line lawyers while Alagna is left without the advice of counsel."

There is no evidence that the Ward Line conspired to frame Alagna. On the contrary, it appears that the Ward Line and Alagna both played completely into Rogers's hands. The Ward Line strategists merely waited with fingers crossed to see what Rogers would tell the investigators, and then waited just as anxiously to see what Alagna would say. It was the net result of these two transcripts of testimony, the one with its "reluctantly offered" information that Alagna was the vengeful one marked for dismissal, and the other with its incriminating evidence against the ship's officers, that forced the Ward Line to go along with Rogers.

There is even reason to believe that the Ward Line could have undermined Rogers's testimony. A man who was intimately and officially connected with the Ward Line throughout the Grand Jury investigation and criminal trial that followed, was recently asked why, during the criminal trial, the prosecution did not call Rogers, the hero of the disaster, to contradict some of Warms's claims about the sending of the S O S. "The prosecution didn't dare call Rogers," this man said. "They knew very well what we could have done to him on the stand."

What did this man mean, except that the Ward Line had information about Rogers that had never been made public? During the several months that elapsed between the disaster and the trial, the prosecution must have found out what the Ward Line had known all along. Otherwise, why wasn't Rogers, the star witness in the Custom House and Grand Jury investigations, called to testify in the criminal trial itself?

It is no wonder that Alagna attempted suicide when the man whose life he had saved, the hero himself, who may have started the fire, managed to enlist even the Ward Line in his attempt to incriminate him. "Some firesetters seem to center their interest in tantalizing the fire investigators and detectives, demonstrating how they can outsmart these officials," Lewis and Yarnell write in *Pathological Firesetting*.

When Rogers told Preston Dillenbeck that he was an "ingenious young man," he had good reason to boast. He had succeeded in deceiving Alagna, the Ward Line, the investigators, the newspapers and the American public. At one point during the Custom House investigation, he was asked how long he had been a maritime radio operator. "Since 1912," he said. A simple check would have shown that in 1912 Rogers was eleven years old. No such check was made, however, because, as the disaster's great hero, he was looked upon as the one man into whose past it would have been a waste of time to look.

Had Preston Dillenbeck come forward in 1934 with the two anonymous letters that Rogers had had him send to Stanley Ferson, the whole investigation might have been centered on Rogers instead of on Alagna against whom evidence was completely lacking. If anyone was investigated thoroughly after the disaster, Alagna was; if there had been evidence to indict him, it would have been done.

An investigation of Rogers's past would have shown that he had been lying and stealing since he was twelve years old. In 1914, he was brought to juvenile court in Oakland, California, for the theft of a wireless receiver set. Placed on parole, he was sent by his grandmother, Gene Dobson Rogers (both parents were dead), to the

Good Templar Home in Vallejo, California, where he was reported to be a "petty thief; very untruthful; a moral pervert."

In 1915, he was again brought to juvenile court and committed to the Boys and Girls Aid society in San Francisco, where he "committed sodomy on a younger boy," and was classified as "thoroughly unreliable."

In 1917, he was paroled to accept a wireless operator's job on a steamship, and two years later he joined the navy. Nine months after his enlistment he was discharged for "dimness of vision" and gravitated back to New York where he was born.

In 1923, he was discharged from his job at WJZ in the Aeolian Building in New York after detectives had questioned him about the thefts of two 50-watt radio tubes valued at $300.

In 1924, he committed "a criminal assault on a ten-year-old boy."

In 1929, the mysterious Wireless Egert Company fire took place at 179 Greenwich Street where Rogers was employed.

In 1930, there was another theft, this time of $2,000 worth of radio laboratory instruments from the L. A. Dussol Company at 135 Liberty Street in New York City. Rogers sold these instruments to the same Wireless Egert Company that had suffered fire damage the year before. He made restitution and was not prosecuted.

The 1934 *Morro Castle* fire followed, and in 1935 there was the fire in Rogers's own radio repair shop in Bayonne, New Jersey.

Rogers was convicted of the attempted murder of Lieutenant Doyle in 1938. The evidence against him was completely circumstantial, but according to the judge who tried the case when Rogers waived a jury trial, there was no room for doubt as to who had sent the bomb to Lieutenant Doyle. Before sentencing him to from twelve to twenty years in the New Jersey State Penitentiary in Trenton, the judge said:

"This was a crime of a diabolical nature, only to be executed by one with the mind of a fiend. There is no doubt in my mind that the finger of guilt points unerringly to you. It has been said that you were the victim of a frame-up on the part of the Bayonne police. There was nothing in the testimony adduced to show this . . ."

In 1942, Rogers, who still had many influential friends believing in his innocence, was given a conditional parole to enter military service. "The armed services need radio men and I want to serve my country," Rogers had told the parole board.

After his release he tried one service and then another, but none would have him. His efforts to enlist took months, however, during which time his behavior was so exemplary that the parole board, on being told by J. B. Duffy of the Radiomarine Corporation of America that a radio operator's job on a freighter would be made available to him, extended his parole.

In *Pathological Firesetting*, Lewis and Yarnell write: "The would-be hero firesetters are motivated primarily by vanity. . . . They are exhibitionists, pathological liars, but withal glib and ingratiating, well thought of by friends and employers. They are convivial fraternizers whom their family or friends will rescue from trouble.

"But they are firesetters, and like all such, there is the other side to their personalities. They are impulsive and unmoral, capable of assault, rape, and thefts. . . .

"As a group they are difficult to convict, as someone invariably appears to plead for them and assumes responsibility for their good behavior on parole. If committed to a hospital, they are usually discharged within a year's time with a diagnosis of psychopathic personality."

After the war, Rogers continued to live in Bayonne, where he often passed Lieutenant Doyle in the street. "I often used to see his red truck go by—it was brand-new—and then look at the stubs of my fingers," Doyle says today.

There were still people in town who believed that the Bayonne police had framed Rogers, and among them were two of Rogers's neighbors on Avenue E, William Hummel, an eighty-three-year-old retired printer for the *Bayonne Times,* and his spinster daughter, Edith. They lived at 582 Avenue E in a two-story clapboard house whose back yard overlooked the Jersey Central's tracks, and Rogers lived across the street and down one block at 601, a corner house hidden behind high hedges and thick shrubbery.

Hummel and Rogers had many of the same hobbies; they were both interested in tape recordings, photography, electrical gadgetry and the Bible. Rogers visited the Hummels often, and when they bought their first television set, it was always Rogers who fixed anything that went wrong.

In 1953, the Hummels put their house up for sale with the intention of going to St. Petersburg, Florida, to live. Rogers by this time owed them over $7,500, and though they intended to collect it, they did not immediately present Rogers with their demands because they were "afraid of what he might do," confronted with the threat of exposure. They had canceled checks to prove their charges, and they and Rogers both knew what the Bayonne police thought of their former patrolman. Over and over again they had advanced Rogers money to help establish him in business, but the war-surplus radio and electrical equipment had either been lost in transit or something unforeseen in the transaction had required that he be advanced more money.

"It may have been unwise on my part to continually

advance Rogers money," Hummel wrote in his records before his death, "but Rogers is very tempermental and I was in constant fear that he might have reneged . . . and I would be in danger of losing everything."

When the Hummel house was sold, the friction and suspicion between Rogers and the Hummels reached a climax. Hummel, still occupying the house at 582 Avenue E, was gradually severing his relations with Bayonne in anticipation of settling in Florida. His most pressing unfinished business was the Rogers debt, which almost equalled the sale price of his house.

One morning Hummel was on his way downtown to the bank when Rogers appeared and offered to drive him. Hummel knew better than to refuse his temperamental neighbor; he went and withdrew $2,000 from the bank.

Sometime in the forty-eight hours following Hummel's return to Avenue E from the bank, he and his daughter were bludgeoned to death in their already-sold home. The murders were separate and distinct; the old man was killed in front of the fireplace downstairs, while the daughter was attacked upstairs in the bathroom, where she fell but somehow found the strength to crawl into her bedroom and under her bed to avoid a second attack. She bled to death there.

Both murders were bloody, and Rogers, who had

worn the same pair of trousers for two years, according to neighbors, suddenly started wearing a different pair. He had been in debt but now began to spend money and to buy radio equipment. One of these purchases he paid for with three one-hundred-dollar bills, the very number that the bank teller in Bayonne remembered having given Hummel prior to his death.

Meanwhile, the Hummels' absence made no one suspicious because their neighbors had been told of their plans to visit relatives. A few days after the murder, however, the pressure began to tell on Rogers. He was paying his regular daily visit to Scheff's Radio Repair Shop in Bayonne, when Scheff's wife, complaining of a leak in the oil line to the stove used to heat the store, began to wipe up a small pool of oil from the floor. The Hummel bodies were still undiscovered, and Rogers, watching Mrs. Scheff mop up the oil, said, "If you'd just drop a match into that, your problems would be solved."

On the seventh day, the sight of the Hummel house across the street and the secret knowledge of the decomposition taking place within proved too much even for Rogers. The compulsion to divulge what no one else knew, like the compulsion to tell Lieutenant Doyle what had caused the *Morro Castle* fire, finally took possession of him.

"There's a mystery in our town," he told Scheff. "The

Hummels left last week to visit relatives in New York. They're supposed to be in Bloomington and they haven't arrived. Nobody has inquired. I wonder why."

Scheff thought no more about it until, five days later, the relatives in Bloomington asked the Bayonne police to investigate and the two bodies were discovered.

During the trial that followed, Rogers's lawyers did not call a single witness, nor did they allow Rogers to testify in his own behalf. The defense, attacking what was again admittedly circumstantial evidence, rested its case on the contention that the murder charge had not been proven.

The jury found Rogers guilty in three hours and twenty minutes but recommended life imprisonment. He was given two concurrent life sentences and sent back to the New Jersey State Penitentiary in Trenton.

When Rogers was interviewed in prison in 1956, he displayed the same calm detachment and unshakable sincerity with which he testified during the *Morro Castle* investigation. At that time, *The New York Times* wrote: "He told his story as impersonally as if it were something that happened to somebody else a long time ago."

Rogers was a great Bible reader and informed interviewers of the fact almost immediately. God would see him through, he'd say, and in the same breath put in a request for some science-fiction pocket books.

"Each day I awaken it is to give honor and glory to God and to Jesus Christ our Lord. It is written, 'God is a very present help in trouble.' It is also written, 'I will not leave thee comfortless, I will come to you.' I believe that. Negative thinking is something I don't practice. Positive thinking is something I do. I never feel sorry for myself. My faith in all things is based on my Christian experience. You can send me money; money orders are best. You can send me five pounds of food a month, only certain things. I'll get you a list. You can send me science fiction, what are called pocket books. No newspapers or magazines except as a subscription direct from the publisher. Science magazines are best."

He seemed to be one of those men who see God as the power in the universe and who spend their lives trying to understand especially the more occult aspects of that power. God was omnipresent, and so was Rogers, since he could both devise bombs and be somewhere else when they exploded. God could see into the future, predict events and play games with time, and so could Rogers in a sense. Religion was an ingenious device, the Bible a kind of Ingersol to tinker with.

Rogers communicated with interviewers by telephone, staring at them through a pane of glass bracketed in concrete. One got the feeling as one looked into his eyes that he really believed, somewhere in the darkness of his mind, that with the Bible and enough science fiction at his side, he would somehow get out of prison.

If an interviewer tried too obviously to elicit information about the *Morro Castle* fire, the information became more scantily offered. Nothing he said seemed in the least incriminating at the time, and it soon became apparent that the gift of a typewriter would have to precede a full discussion of the part he played in the disaster.

"The permitted one is Remington Quiet Writer—Pica type. It must be shipped directly from the place of purchase, and must have their shipping label on the package. It must be new and come direct from them. By Railway Express preferably. Have it sent soon before there is an embargo on them here."

Next to the typewriter, he talked mostly about his innocence. The Bayonne police had framed him in both the Doyle bombing case and the Hummel murder case, he said. "William and Edith Hummel were my dearest friends. How could I have killed them? I've never harmed anyone. I'm innocent."

His confidential manner—the earnestness with which he asked that the Court of Last Resort be brought into the case on his behalf—eventually accentuated his lack of humanity. The Court of Last Resort would investigate the Hummel murder, he said, and see to it that he got another trial.

It was at this moment, in 1956, on the basis of what was then admittedly hearsay and rumor, that Rogers was suddenly asked, "Did you start the *Morro Castle* fire?"

Rogers's eyes were the most impressive thing about him. They seemed in touch with two or three different minds instead of the usual one. They grew dark and angry at the question, but then, almost immediately, a smile played on his lips and he said, "What about the Court of Last Resort?"

As that smile was interpreted, he was saying, "If my case is brought before the Court of Last Resort, and that fails, I'll tell everything."

But his case was never brought before the Court of Last Resort, and on January 10, 1958, he died of a stroke in the New Jersey State Penitentiary in Trenton.

ACKNOWLEDGMENTS

The author wishes to express his appreciation to the survivors of the *Morro Castle* who gave their time and effort during interviews, and a special indebtedness to the following for invaluable help, suggestions and information:

GEORGE ALAGNA
      Former First Assistant Radio Operator, *Morro Castle*
DR. S. JOSEPH BREGSTEIN
      First President, *Morro Castle* Association
CAPTAIN C. H. BROACH
      U. S. Coast Guard, Washington, D. C.
ROBERT N. CALDWELL
      Editor, *Bayonne Times,* New Jersey

Joseph Curran
    President, National Maritime Union
Rear Admiral Ben Scott Custer
    U. S. Navy. Retired
Captain Vincent J. Doyle
    Bayonne Police, New Jersey
Warden George F. Goodman
    New Jersey State Penitentiary
Deputy Chief Fire Marshal John J. Gribbon
    New York City
Charles W. Hagen
    Attorney-at-Law
Kenneth R. Hall
    Archivist, Industrial Records Branch
    The National Archives, Washington, D. C.
Lieutenant Commander Howard H. Hansen
    U. S. Navy. Retired
Associate Dean George W. Hibbitt
    Columbia University
Harold E. Hufford
    Archivist-in-Charge, Legislative Branch
    The National Archives, Washington, D. C.
Toussaint Prince
    Archivist, Legislative Branch
    The National Archives, Washington, D. C.
Mrs. Frances B. Ryan
    Assistant to Warden
    New Jersey State Penitentiary
Commander W. R. Sayer
    U. S. Coast Guard, Washington, D. C.

PASSENGER LIST

ADAMS, MISS JANE, Philadelphia, Pa., bruises, shock and submersion
AGUIAR, VAL
ALTENBURG, MRS. S., Brooklyn, N. Y., drowned
ARNETH, PAUL, Brooklyn, N. Y., shock and burns
ASCHOFF, MR. and MRS. THORPE H., Flushing, N. Y., submersion
ATROMEZ, GEORGE
ATICELLO, MARCO
BADER, CHARLES, Baldwin, L. I., N. Y., drowned
BAHRINGER, MRS. JULIA, Scarborough, N. Y., drowned
BAHRINGER, MISS LILLIAN, Scarborough, N. Y., drowned
BARNSTEAD, MR. and MRS. LLOYD C., Bronx, N. Y.
BARRIOS, ANTIRO, Brooklyn, N. Y.
BEACH, AGNES
BEHLING, MISS ANNE, Philadelphia, Pa., drowned

BEHR, CHARLES, Brooklyn, N. Y.

BEHR, MISS ETHEL, Brooklyn, N. Y.

BARRY, MISS A.

BERGENSTEIN, MISS DOROTHY

BERLINER, M., fatally burned

BIREN, MISS ROSE, Philadelphia, Pa., burns, submersion and shock

BLANCO, BOB

BLONDEAU, DR. and MRS. JULES, Philadelphia, Pa., shock and submersion

BLOODGOOD, MARJORIE, Hillside, N. J.

BODNER, MR. and MRS. STEPHEN, Elizabeth, N. J., burns, shock

BORNELL, MR. and MRS. J. H.

BORMAN, HARRY, Freeport, L. I., N. Y.

BRADY, EDWARD J., Philadelphia, Pa., drowned

BRADY, MRS. EDWARD, Philadelphia, Pa., severe shock

BRADY, MISS NANCY, Philadelphia, Pa., shock and submersion

BRADBURY, MISS MARTHA, Wetherly, Pa., immersion, shock

BREGSTEIN, DR. S. JOSEPH, Brooklyn, N. Y.

BREGSTEIN, MASTER MERVIN G., Brooklyn, N. Y., drowned

BRENNAN, MISS ELEANOR, Bronx, N. Y., drowned

BREWER, HARRY, Brooklyn, N. Y.

BRINKMAN, DR. and MRS. HARRY, Bellerose, L. I., N. Y.

BRODIE, MISS HELEN, Hartford, Conn., pneumonia, shock

BROWN, MISS FLORENCE, N. Y. C.

BROWN, MISS IDA, Brooklyn, N. Y.

BROWN, MRS. HARRIET, Philadelphia, Pa., burns, shock

BROWNEY, MISS G.

BUDLONG, MISS MARJORIE, exposure and shock

BURRELL, DR. JAMES, Buffalo, N. Y.

BURRELL, MRS. JAMES, Buffalo, N. Y., drowned

BUSQUET, DR. FRANÇOIS A., Havana, Cuba, drowned

BUSQUET, MRS. F., Havana, Cuba

BUSQUET, MISS OPHELIA, Havana, Cuba

BUTTE, JAMES, Brooklyn, N. Y.

Byrne, Mrs. John T., Richmond Hill, N. Y., drowned

Byrne, Walter E., Caldwell, N. J., burns

Caleya, Juan

Canavan, Miss Katherine, Brooklyn, N. Y., immersion

Cannon, Thomas, Livingston, N. J.

Capote, Renee, Havana, Cuba

Carpenter, Miss Madge, Queens, N. Y.

Casey, Miss Carolyn, Philadelphia, Pa., shock, immersion

Chalfont, John, 2nd., Wayne, Pa.

Chalfont, Miss L., Wayne, Pa.

Chesler, Miss Estelle, Brooklyn, N. Y., burns, immersion

Clark, William, Howard Beach, Queens, N. Y., burns of eyes
and throat

Clark, Frank, Howard Beach, Queens, N. Y., exposure, exhaustion

Clark, Mrs. Carrie J., Howard Beach, Queens, N. Y., drowned

Cochrane, Catherine N., Brooklyn, N. Y., fatally burned

Cochrane, Dr. Charles, Brooklyn, N. Y.

Cohen, Abraham, Hartford, Conn., burns, immersion

Cohen, Mrs. Abraham, Hartford, Conn., shock, immersion

Cohn, Miss Gertrude, N. Y. C., immersion

Coll, Dr. James P., Jersey City, N. J., drowned

Coll, Mrs. James, Jersey City, N. J., severe shock

Coll, Miss Dorothy, Jersey City, N. J., exposure

Comacho, Rosario, Havana, Cuba

Conroy, Miss Cornelia R., Baltimore, Md., drowned

Conroy, Miss Ann, Philadelphia, Pa.

Conway, Miss Anne

Cotter, Miss Margaret, Springfield, Mass., shock

Cullen, Miss Una, Brooklyn, N. Y., immersion

Davis, Mrs. Minnie, Brooklyn, N. Y., burns, both legs; fracture,
right shoulder

Davis, Miss Anne, Brooklyn, N. Y., immersion

Davidson, Miss Lillian, Clifton, N. J., immersion, overcome by
shock

Davidson, Mr. and Mrs. Sydney, Brooklyn, N. Y.

DESVERNINE, MISSES MADELINE and ALICE, Tuckahoe, N. Y., immersion

DILLON, MRS. JAMES, Brooklyn, N. Y., drowned

DISTLER, LOUIS, Brooklyn, N. Y., drowned

DISTLER, ADELAIDE, Brooklyn, N. Y., drowned

DITTMAN, FRANK, N. Y. C., immersion

D'ORN, MRS. ANGELA, Havana, Cuba

DRUMMOND, MR. and MRS. J. A., Philadelphia, Pa.

DULK, MICHAEL, N. Y. C., inflammation of eyes

EGAN, FATHER RAYMOND, N. Y. C., burns on hands and face

EGELHOFF, GEORGE T.

EHERMAN, MISS MARJORIE, Hempstead, L. I., N. Y., shock, immersion

ELIAS, CHARLES, Paterson, New Jersey, drowned

ENGLISH, GEORGE A., Lynbrook, L. I., N. Y.

ERRICKSON, MISS JERRY, Flushing, Queens, N. Y., drowned

FABEL, MISS C.

FAULCONER, FRED C., Alexandria, Va., drowned

FEATHERSTON, THOMAS M., Wilkes-Barre, Pa., drowned

FEINBERG, NATHAN, N. Y. C.

FELIPE, MISS ROSARIO, N. Y. C., burns of thigh and both arms

FERGENSTEIN, MISS DOROTHY, N. Y. C., immersion

FILSTER, CHARLES P., Jamaica, Queens, N. Y., drowned

FILSTER, MRS. CHARLES, Queens, N. Y.

FITZGERALD, MISS GRACE G., N. Y. C., smoke in lungs

FITZGERALD, MISS EVELYN, Worcester, Mass., shock, immersion

FISH, MISS E.

FLYNN, JAMES, Jersey City, N. J.

FOLKMAN, MISS SYDNEY, N. Y. C., immersion

FREIRE, JOSEPH, Santiago, Cuba, immersion

FRIEND, MISS L.

FRYMAN, MISS FANNIE, Philadelphia, Pa., drowned

GEFFERT, MR. and MRS. PHILIP, Jersey City, N. J., shock

GIANNINI, DR. and MRS. PAUL, Point Pleasant, N. J., shock, exposure

GILLIGAN, MISS MARIE, Philadelphia, Pa., immersion

GILLIGAN, MISS REGINA, Philadelphia, Pa., immersion

GILMORE, MISS MARY, Bronx, N. Y., multiple second-degree burns of both legs and arms

GIRO, DR. EMILIO, Santiago, Cuba, shock

GOLDEN, WILLIAM, Caldwell, N. J., immersion

GONZALEZ, ROBERTO, Newburgh, N. Y., drowned

GRIESNER, FREDERICK, Brooklyn, N. Y., drowned

GRIESNER, MRS. FREDERICK, Brooklyn, N. Y., drowned

GRIESNER, MRS. AUGUSTA (mother of Frederick), Brooklyn, N. Y., drowned

GRIMM, WILLIAM, drowned

HAESSLER, WILLIAM, Queens, N. Y., died of lobar pneumonia

HAGEDORN, HENRY, Brooklyn, N. Y., drowned

HAGEDORN, MRS. MINNIE, Brooklyn, N. Y., drowned

HASSALL, JAMES, Forest Hills, N. Y.

HASSALL, MRS. JAMES, Forest Hills, N. Y.

HASSALL, MISS LORETTA, Forest Hills, N. Y., burns on foot, laceration of thigh

HEIMAN, JOSEPH, N. Y. C., drowned

HELM, NAN, Summit, N. J., burns on hands

HENRICKS, MISS E., Philadelphia, Pa.

HIDALGO, JOSE, Havana, Cuba

HILL, MISS ALMA, Philadelphia, Pa.

HIRSCH, BENJAMIN, Philadelphia, Pa., shock, immersion

HIRSCH, MRS. B., Philadelphia, Pa., shock, immersion

HOED, FRANCESCO, Havana, Cuba, drowned

HOFMAN, C., drowned

HOFFMAN, MISS DORA, Queens, N. Y., burns and lacerations of both legs

HOFFMAN, CHARLES, Queens, N. Y.

HOFFMAN, MISS EVA, London, Ontario, Canada, drowned

HOLDEN, RUBEN A., Cincinnati, Ohio, severe shock, exhaustion

HOLDEN, MRS. RUBEN, Cincinnati, Ohio, drowned

HOLDEN, JOHN AND RUBEN, Cincinnati, Ohio, exposure, severe shock

HOSANKE, MISS H.

HULL, Miss Edith, N. Y. C., injured back
HULSE, Hiram, Havana, Cuba, shock, exposure
HULSE, Mrs. Hiram, Havana, Cuba, shock, exposure
JAKOBY, Henry, Brooklyn, N. Y., drowned
JAKOBY, Mrs. Henry, Brooklyn, N. Y.
JAKOBY, Henry, Jr., Brooklyn, N. Y., drowned
JOHNSON, Miss Edna M., Brooklyn, N. Y., exposure
KEDY, Wilfred, Hotel Pennsylvania, N. Y. C., lacerations and shock
KEMPF, John, Queens, N. Y., exposure, immersion
KENDALL, Edward, Pt. Pleasant, N. J., burns, cuts, exposure
KENNEDY, James F., Hamilton Beach, Queens, N. Y., drowned
KENNEDY, Mrs. James, Hamilton Beach, Queens, N. Y., severe shock
KENT, John S., Swarthmore, Pa., drowned
KIRBY, Sara, Brooklyn, N. Y., burns and bruises
KLEIN, Milton, Paterson, N. J., drowned
KLEINBERG, Miss Karin, Spring Lake, N. J., exposure, immersion
KNIGHT, Miss Gladys, Shrewsbury, Mass., complete exhaustion and exposure
KNIGHT, Miss Ethel, Shrewsbury, Mass., complete exhaustion and exposure
KOSBOTHE, Adolphe E., Brooklyn, N. Y., drowned
KOSBOTHE, Mrs. Mary, Brooklyn, N. Y., drowned
KRAUS, Miss Rose, N. Y. C., drowned
KUHN, Mrs. Anne, Lynbrook, L. I., N. Y., drowned
KURLAND, Miss Pauline, shock
LANDAU, Miss Dorothy, Queens, N. Y., submersion, shock
LAMBER, Oscar
LANDMANN, Mr. and Mrs. Clementes, Matanzas, Cuba, exposure
LANDMANN, Miss, Matanzas, Cuba, shock
LAMPE, Mr. and Mrs. Emil, Brooklyn, N. Y., shock, submersion
LANDIS, Miss Doris, Queens, N. Y., shock, submersion
LA ROCHE, Miss Florence, Providence, R. I., shock and cut on head

LEMPRECHT, MR. AND MRS. PAUL, Jersey City, N. J., exposure, shock

LEVY, MISS DIANA, Bronx, N. Y., cuts, burns, shock

LERNER, DR. and MRS. SAMUEL, Brooklyn, N. Y., shock, exposure

LIEBER, MISS KATHERINE, Queens, New York, shock, submersion

LIKEWISE, JACOB, Brooklyn, N. Y., drowned

LIKEWISE, MRS. JACOB, Brooklyn, N. Y., severe shock, exhaustion

LIONE, ANTHONY, Sunnyside, Queens, N. Y., drowned

LIONE, MRS. ANTHONY, Sunnyside, Queens, N. Y., burns, submersion, shock

LIONE, MASTER ROBERT, Sunnyside, Queens, N. Y., severe shock

LIONE, RAYMOND, Queens, N. Y., drowned

LISPCOMB, HARRY A., Alexandria, Va., drowned

LISTIO, MILTON, Worcester, Mass., drowned

LITVAK, MISS ANN G., Philadelphia, Pa., drowned

LOFMARK, MRS. DOROTHY H., N. Y. C., drowned

LOHR, MRS. LETTY C., Brooklyn, N. Y., drowned

LOMSE, MRS. M., drowned

LONGE, MRS. MYETT, Queens, N. Y., shock

LOVELAND, FRANK, Billerica, Mass., burns about eyes and shock

LOVELAND, MRS. FRANK, Billerica, Mass., shock, submersion

LYON, MORTON, JR., Wayne, Pa., drowned

MALONEY, MISS MAE, Brooklyn, N. Y., exposure and shock

MALONEY, MRS., Brooklyn, N. Y.

MARSHALL, MRS. NELLIE, Brooklyn, N. Y., drowned

MARQUARD, MISS BERTHA, St. Albans, N. Y., submersion and exhaustion

MARQUARD, GUSTAVE, St. Albans, N. Y., burns and exposure

MAYER, MISS H.

MAYER, HERMAN, exhaustion

MAYER, MRS. SOPHIE, shock and submersion

McARTHUR, ALEXANDER, Philadelphia, Pa., drowned

McARTHUR, MRS. ALEXANDER, Philadelphia, Pa., severe shock

MEISSNER, ROBERT O., Queens, N. Y., exposure and shock

MEISSNER, MRS. ROBERT O., Queens, N. Y., submersion, severe shock

MELEY, FRANK B., East Orange, N. J., drowned

MENKEN, MR. and MRS. CHARLES, Brooklyn, N. Y., exposure, submersion, shock

MESTRE, RAFAEL, Santiago, Cuba, injured

MILLER, MRS. ALICE, Hartford, Conn., exposure, shock

MILLER, ADELAIDE, Hartford, Conn., exposure, shock

MILLER, MR. and MRS. H. C., N. Y. C.

McELHENY, MATTHEW L., Plainfield, N. J., exposure

MILLIKEN, MRS. MARIE, Brooklyn, N. Y.

MORAN, MRS. EMILY, Brooklyn, N. Y., drowned

MORAN, MISS MARIAN, Brooklyn, N. Y., drowned

MULLER, FRANCES, Hempstead, L. I., N. Y., drowned

MULLER, HERMAN, Queens, N. Y., exposure, shock

MULLER, MISS D., Spring Lake, N. J., submersion, bruises

MULLER, MISS H., Spring Lake, N. J., submersion, bruises

MURPHY, MISS SARAH R., Philadelphia, Pa., multiple contusions of both legs and left arm

MURPHY, MISS FRANCES, Germantown, Pa., first-degree burns of face and shock

MURPHY, MRS. FRANCES, Germantown, Pa., fatally burned

NASS, MRS. FRANCIS, Philadelphia, Pa., shock, submersion and smoke

NATHANSON, MISS Z.

NEWMARK, PHILIP, Brooklyn, N. Y., severe shock

NEWMARK, MRS. D., Brooklyn, N. Y., drowned

NOTEBOOM, MISS KAY, Brooklyn, N. Y., shock

O'CONNER, CHARLES, Brooklyn, N. Y., injuries of face and scalp

OLMSTEAD, MRS. R., shock, submersion

OLESON, MRS. LAURA, Westerleigh, S. I., N. Y., drowned

OVERGENE, MISS L., drowned

PANINI, MR. and MRS. HERMAN, Bangor, Pa., shock, submersion and exhaustion

PERLMAN, BESSIE, Brooklyn, N. Y., drowned

PELLICE, MRS. VIOLA, Brooklyn, N. Y., drowned

PELLICE, LOUIS, Brooklyn, N. Y., drowned

PERRONE, LEWIS, Princeton, N. J.

PETREE, JAMES, Jackson Heights, N. Y., fractured leg
PHELPS, DR. and MRS. GOUVERNEUR MORRIS, N. Y. C.
PHELPS, G. M., JR., N. Y. C., exhaustion, exposure
PIEDRA, AURELIO, Havana, Cuba
PIERCE, T. M.
POTTBERG, EARNEST E., West New Brighton, S. I., N. Y., drowned
PRESCOTT, DONALD, Bridgeford, N. D.
PRICE, WILLIAM F., N. Y. C., severe shock, exhaustion
PRICE, MRS. MARY E., N. Y. C., drowned
PRINCE, MISS AGNES M., Pottstown, Pa., immersion, exhaustion
PRINCE, MISS RUTH, Pottstown, Pa., immersion, exhaustion
PRUZAN, MISS JEANETTE, N. Y. C., bruises, burns, shock
PUSRIN, MISS AUGUSTA, Pinehurst, N. J., shock
REINEKINS, MRS. FORD, drowned
RIENZ, MARTIN, Brooklyn, N. Y.
RIENZ, MRS. MARIE, Brooklyn, N. Y., drowned
RIDDERHOFF, GEORGE
ROBINSON, MRS. R., Richmond Hill, N. Y.
ROBINSON, MISS L., Richmond Hill, N. Y.
ROBERTS, MRS. BETTY, Pawtucket, R. I., exposure, shock
ROBERTS, MISS FLORENCE, Pawtucket, R. I., exposure, shock
RUDBERG, ISRAEL, Shenandoah, Pa., shock and bruises
RUEDA, MASTER BENITO, N. Y. C., exhaustion, shock
RUEDA, MRS. JULIA, N. Y. C., shock and submersion
RUEDA, DICKIE, N. Y. C., drowned
SAENZ, MISS CAINA, Havana, Cuba, drowned
SAENZ, MISS MARTHA, Havana, Cuba, drowned
SAENZ, MRS. MARGUERITE, Havana, Cuba, fatally burned
SAENZ, MASTER BRAULIO, Havana, Cuba, fatally burned
SAGEMAN, MRS. A.
SCHEELY, AUGUST, Glendale, L. I., N. Y., severe shock
SCHEELY, MRS. AUGUST, Glendale, L. I., N. Y., drowned
SCHMITT, MISS M.
SCHMITT, MISS E.
SCHNEIDER, DAVID, shock

SHERIDAN, MRS. JAMES, Wilkes-Barre, Pa., severe shock, submersion

SHERIDAN, MASTER ARTHUR D., Wilkes-Barre, Pa., drowned

SHERMAN, MISS FLORENCE, Philadelphia, Pa., shock and submersion

SIGMUND, MISS CLARA, Bardonia, N. Y., bruises, cuts, shock

SIVATION, A. R.

SLACK, MISS MARION, bruises and congestion of lungs

SPECTOR, FRANCES, Brooklyn, N. Y., drowned

STECKLO, MRS. MARY, N. Y. C., exposure, exhaustion

STEMMERMAN, MISS ANN, Queens, N. Y., lacerations of head

STEWARD, FRANCIS, N. Y. C., drowned

STRAUCH, DR. HENRY J., Donora, Pa., drowned

STRAUCH, MRS. HENRY J., Donora, Pa., drowned

STABNER, MRS. SARAH E., Queens, N. Y., fractured hips

SUHR, MISS ELSIE, N. Y. C., shock, exposure

SUAREZ Y MURIAS, EDUARDO, Havana, Cuba, drowned

TAUBERT, MISS LOUISE, Providence, Rhode Island, drowned

THOMPSON, MISS ELMIRA, Brooklyn, N. Y., shock, exposure

THRON, MISS S., drowned

TORBORG, HERMAN, Brooklyn, N. Y., exposure, exhaustion

TORBORG, JOHN, Brooklyn, N. Y., exposure, exhaustion

TORBORG, MISS RUTH, Brooklyn, N. Y., shock, submersion

TOSTI, FRANK, N. Y. C., drowned

VALLEJO, MISS JULIA, Queens, N. Y., bruises, cuts, exposure

VERJENSTEIN, MISS D.

VOGT, MISS LOUISE AGNES, Brooklyn, N. Y., drowned

VOSSELER, DR. THEODORE L., Brooklyn, N. Y.

VOSSELER, MRS. THEODORE, Brooklyn, N. Y.

VON VLINTZ, MRS. E.

VILLEHOZ, DRENA, drowned

VITALE, SAMUEL, Detroit, Michigan, exhaustion, shock

VITALE, MRS. SAMUEL, Detroit, Michigan, exhaustion, shock

WACKER, MISS DORIS, Roselle Park, N. J.

WACKER, HERBERT J., Roselle Park, N. J., drowned

WACKER, MRS. HERBERT, Roselle Park, N. J.

WALD, MISS SADIE, N. Y. C., shock and eye burns

WALLACE, MISS ADELE, Hartford, Conn., shock, exposure, burns

WECKER, HENRIETTA, Brooklyn, N. Y., drowned

WEIL, WILLIAM H., N. Y.

WEIL, MRS. WILLIAM H., N. Y., drowned

WEINBERGER, EMANUEL, Philadelphia, Pa., fracture of right shoulder

WEINBERGER, MRS. EMANUEL, Philadelphia, Pa., severe shock, exposure

WEINTRAUB, MISS BESSIE, Brooklyn, N. Y., shock, exposure

WEISER, MISS IDA, Brooklyn, N. Y., bruises, shock, exposure

WEISER, PHILIP, Brooklyn, N. Y., exhaustion, submersion

WEISER, MRS. PHILIP, Brooklyn, N. Y., exhaustion, submersion

WHEELER, MISS EVELYN, Spring Lake, N. J., exposure, submersion, exhaustion

WHITLOCK, GEORGE, Great Neck, L. I., N. Y., exhaustion

WHITLOCK, MRS. G., Great Neck, L. I., N. Y., exposure and chill

WILLIAMS, HELEN, Scranton, Pa., exposure, laceration, shock

ZIMPLINSKI, HENRY F., Brooklyn, N. Y., drowned

CREW LIST

ABBOTT, EBAN S., chief engineer
ABBOTT, ERNEST, junior engineer
ALAGNA, GEORGE, second radio operator
ALUMTIS, ANTONIO, second cook
ALVAREZ, CARLOS, bedroom steward, drowned
ANGELO, CHARLES, ordinary seaman
ANZALONE, CHARLES, able seaman
APICELLA, MARCO, gymnasium instructor
AZAGUIRRE, ANSELMO, third cook
BAGLEY, ARTHUR, ordinary seaman
BALLEJO, ANTONIO, linekeeper
BARRIOS, ARTURO, sculleryman, drowned
BARROS, IVAN, fireman
BATTELLA, DONATA, oiler
BEAUMONT, ELLIS, wiper
BECK, LENA, stewardess

BENDET, MAX, musician
BERESFORD, ROBERT, seaman
BERNHARDT, WILLIAM, able seaman
BERTO, J., deck steward, drowned
BERTOCI, JAMES, steward
BICKEL, WILLIAM, assistant cruise director
BILBAO, PHILIP, bedroom steward
BOGETTI, SIREL, deck steward
BOGUSON, ELIAS, drowned
BOSKO, JOSEPH
BRADKIN, IRVING, musician, drowned
BRINK, CHARLES, deck pantryman
BROWN, MRS. HARRIET, stewardess
BRUNS, GEORGE, waiter
BUJIA, ANTONIO, first engineer
BURGESS, GENE, fireman's messman
CAFFEY, JOHN, telephone operator
CALDWELL, JOHN, waiter
CAMPA, JOHN, seaman
CAMPBELL, DANIEL, steward
CARDELLICHIO, FRANK, barber, drowned
CARY, FRANK, waiter
CASINIERE, ALBERT, pantryman, drowned
CAULEY, JOHN, elevator operator
CAYHUE, RAYMOND, bath steward
CELLI, NAT, waiter
CHARLES, THOMAS, able seaman
CLAVARRIA, RENEE, bath steward
CLODY, WALTER, seaman
CLUTHE, HERMAN, assistant cruise director
CODY, WALTER, J., JR., cadet
COH, IRVING, engineer cadet
COSTA, ENRIQUE, mess officer
COTE, ROBERT, waiter
CURRY, FRANK, waiter
DALY, ADDIS, elevator operator

DAVIS, JOSEPH, waiter
DAVIS, SYDNEY, bellboy
DERRINGH, WILLIAM, waiter
DINNE, JOHN, quartermaster
DOUGLAS, HERBERT, waiter
DRISCOLL, JAMES, waiter
DUNHAUPT, OTTO, printer
DUNN, GERALD [JERRY], ordinary seaman
D'UVA, JOHN, steward
DU VINAGE, RUSSELL, first assistant purser
ECKLUND, ALBERT, deck steward
EDGERTON, JERRY
EICHLER, CHARLES, steward
ESTRADA, FAUSTINO
FARNELL, HARRY F., drowned
FELIGO, JOHN, sculleryman
FERGUSON, MALCOLM, waiter
FERNANDEZ, JOSEPH, waiter
FERNER, RAMON, wiper, drowned
FERRE, JOSEPH, bedroom steward
FLEISCHMAN, LOUIS, quartermaster
FLOOD, JOHN, fireman
FOERSCH, HAROLD, watchman, drowned
FRANK, HARRY, seaman
FREEMAN, IVAN, second officer [acting first]
FUL, MANUEL, mess officer
GARCIA, FRANCISCO, sculleryman
GARCIA, JOSE, carpenter
GARCIA, MANUEL, storekeeper
GARNER, ROBERT, wiper, drowned
GASCH, ALBERT, bedroom steward
GAZAMBRIDGE, HIRAM, steward
GEORGIO, ANTONIO, oiler
GOETZ, PAUL, chief pantryman
GOMEZ, MANUEL, fifth cook, drowned
GONZALES, GEORGE, cook

GRAHAM, BROOKS, messman, officers' messroom
GROSS, JOHN, able seaman
GUTERBAY, JESUS, sixth cook, drowned
HACKNEY, CLARENCE, third officer [acting second]
HALVORSEN, MISS AAGOT, drowned
HAMEL, RICHARD
HANSEN, HOWARD, fourth officer [acting third]
HARRISON, HENRY, third electrician
HASSIN, MAX, waiter
HENDERSON, SINCLAIR, telephone operator
HERSCHKOWITZ, HARRY, musician
HILL, RAPHAEL, fourth officer
HILLSTRAND, WILLIAM, cadet engineer, drowned
HOFFMAN, SAMUEL, quartermaster
HOUSTON, COLIN, fireman
HOWELL, JOHN, bellboy
INNERKEN, ALBERT, silver steward
IZAGUIRRE, FLORENCIO, chief cook
JACOBY, ELLA, manicurist
JACKSON, CHARLES, wiper
JAMSEN, EDWARD, sculleryman
JOHNSON, TRYGUE, assistant chief carpenter
JUSTIS, WILLIAM, chief electrician
KAPAA, NICHOLAS, fireman
KELSEY, LEROY, able seaman
KIRBY, SARAH, stewardess
KIRKLAND, ALBERT, drowned
KITCHIN, WILLIAM, plumber
KLINGER, GUSTAVE, junior engineer
KLUGER, GUSTAVE, seaman
KONDEROUSIS, DEMOS, water tender
KOPF, RICHARD, waiter
KRUSKE, PETER, portman
LA FUENTA, JESUS, assistant butcher
LARRINGAGA, NICHOLAS, drowned
LATTA, CLYDE, clerk, drowned

LIDELL, CHARLES, steward
LIVINGSTON, SOLOMON, watchman
LOCHMAYER, WILLIAM, ordinary seaman
LOPEZ, JOHN, fourth cook, drowned
MACARSKI, STANLEY, sculleryman, drowned
MAKI, CHARLES, third radio operator
MARTIN, NELSON, waiter, drowned
MARTINEZ, MANUEL, refrigerating engineer
MATA, ANTONIO, messman
MATARRITA, ARTURO, drowned
MAUS, JULIUS, elevator operator, drowned
MAZEN, BEN, waiter
McCRODDON, MICHAEL, waiter
McMANUS, JAMES P., ordinary seaman
McNALLY, BERNARD, storekeeper
MEISNER, R.
MEISNER, MRS. R.
MELBARD, MARTIN, junior engineer
MILLER, ISIDORE, ballroom steward
MILLER, SOL, waiter
MILLER, PERCY, second electrician
MILLNER, ROBERT, ordinary seaman, drowned
MOLNAR, PAUL, bellboy
MONROE, CLARENCE, able seaman
MOORE, ROBERT, wiper
MORRIS, STANLEY, junior engineer, drowned
MUIR, PHILIP, tearoom steward
MONTABOULAS, JAMES, oiler
MULLE, PERCY, electrician
MUNOZ, ANTHONY, waiter
NAVAS, THOMAS, fireman
NEMORESKEY, MORRIS, waiter
NUNNZ, VALENTINE, messman
O'CONNOR, JOSEPH, watchman
OLAVARRIA, RENEE, bath steward, drowned
O'SULLIVAN, WILLIAM, deck storekeeper

OTTENS, HERMAN, waiter
PAZ, MARCELLINO, steward
PENDER, ARTHUR J., watchman
PETTY, SAM, waiter, drowned
PIERCE, THOMAS
POLIGASTRO, GUIDO, bedroom steward, drowned
POND, JAMES, second steward
PRYOR, BILL, waiter
QUITROTO, FELIX, bedroom steward
RAMOS, LUCIANO, bedroom steward, drowned
REICHELE, EUGENE, electrician, drowned
ROBERTS, REGINALD B., oiler
RODRIGUES, FLORENCIO, bath steward
ROGERS, GEORGE, chief radio operator
ROSEN, JULIUS, musician
ROY, JULIAN C.
ROSS, ALEXANDER, cadet, drowned
RUEGG, JOSEPH, third steward
RUSCOE, NELSON, musician
RUSSELL, AUBREY, second engineer
RUSSELL, DIWANACH, assistant purser
RYAN, SYDNEY, deck steward, drowned
SAFFIR, SEYMOUR, bellboy
SALDANA, WILLIAM, bedroom steward
SCHWARTZ, MRS. LENA, stewardess
SEIJO, FELIX, waiter
SHINDEL, GEORGE, chief baker
SMITH, JOHN, bedroom steward
SMITH, ROBERT, cruise director
SOLTIS, JOHN, wiper
SOREL, ALBERT, able seaman
SORIANO, ISAAC, bedroom steward
SPAGNA, JOSEPH, pantryman
SPAGNA, RUSSELL, kitchen helper
SPEIERMAN, HENRY, chief steward
SPILLGAS, JOSEPH, able seaman

STAFFORD, —— (?)

STAMM, HANS, waiter

STAMM, HENRY L., telephone operator

STAMPER, ARTHUR, third engineer

STEVENSON, MILTON, waiter

STUEBER, HARRY, wiper

SUAREZ, FRANCISCO, sculleryman

SUNKENS, WALTER, oiler

SUHR, MISS E.

TANNENBAUM, WILLIAM, steward

THOMAS, JAMES, able seaman, drowned

TOLMAN, ROBERT, purser

TORRES, WILLIAM, able seaman

TORRESSON, THOMAS, third assistant purser

TORREALDAU, CIRIACO, butcher

TRIPP, WILLIAM, cadet engineer

TRUJILLO, LUPENCENO, assistant chief pantryman, drowned

ULRICH, ERNEST, boatswain, drowned

VALLEJO, ANTONIO, linekeeper, drowned

VAN ZILE, DR. DE WITT C., senior surgeon, drowned

VASQUEZ, JOSE, sculleryman

VASSILIADES, JOHN, waiter

VERGUEZ, JOSEPH

VINCK, DAVID, porter

VIOLA, ROCCO, third pantryman

WALTHER, FRED, ordinary seaman

WARMS, WILLIAM F., chief officer

WEBERMAN, GEORGE, baker, drowned

WEBB, GEORGE, fourth engineer

WELCH, JOSEPH, able seaman

WEIDENER, PAUL, officers' messman

WEINTRAUB, WILLIAM, musician

WEISBERGER, MORRIS, able seaman

WILMOTT, ROBERT, captain

WILSON, RICHARD, junior engineer, drowned

WITHERSPOON, NORMAN, waiter

WRIGHT, CHARLES, headwaiter
WRIGHT, LEWIS, junior engineer
WRIGHT, WILLIAM, wiper
YANES, PEDRO, elevator operator
YORK, JAMES, oiler
ZARB, FERDINAND
ZABELLA, ANDREW, fireman
ZABOLA, RAGNE, stewardess, drowned

Total Dead   134 (official count)